CARL AND THE COTTON GIN

Also by Sara Ware Bassett

<table>
<tr><td>THE YOUNG ENGINEERS</td><td>THE STORY OF</td></tr>
<tr><td>Carl and the Cotton Gin</td><td>The Story of Glass</td></tr>
<tr><td>Christopher and the
    Clockmakers</td><td>The Story of Leather
The Story of Silk</td></tr>
<tr><td>Paul and the Printing Press</td><td>The Story of Sugar</td></tr>
<tr><td>Steve and the Steam Engine</td><td>The Story of Porcelain</td></tr>
<tr><td>Ted and the Telephone</td><td>The Story of Lumber</td></tr>
<tr><td>Walter and the Wireless</td><td>The Story of Wool</td></tr>
</table>

This edition published 2026
by Living Book Press

ISBN: 978-1-76153-450-8 (hardcover)
           978-1-76153-452-2 (softcover)

First published in 1924.

This edition is based on the Little, Brown, and Company printing by 1924.

A catalogue record for this
book is available from the
National Library of Australia

CARL AND THE COTTON GIN

by

SARA WARE BASSETT

LIVING BOOK PRESS

"MR. CARL McGREGOR," ANNOUNCED HE IN A STENTORIAN TONE.

Contents

THE McGREGORS

"Carl!"

"Coming, Ma!"

Mrs. McGregor waited a moment.

"But you aren't coming," protested she fretfully. "You never seem to come when you're wanted. Drat the child! Where is he? Carl!"

"Yes, Ma."

"*Yes, Ma! Yes, Ma!*" the woman mimicked impatiently. "It's easy enough to shout *Yes, Ma*; but where are you—that's what I want to know. You're the slowest creature on God's earth, I believe. A tortoise would be a race horse compared with you. What under the sun are you doing?"

The boy entered, a good-humored grin on his face.

He was thin, lanky, and blue-eyed, and a rebellious lock of tawny hair that curled despite all he could do waved back from his forehead. He might have been fourteen years old or he might have been seventeen; it was hard to tell whether he was an overgrown younger boy or an under-sized older one. Whatever his age, however, he could certainly boast a serene disposition, for his mother's caustic comments failed to ruffle his temper. Having heard them ever since babyhood he was quite accustomed to their acid tang; moreover, he had learned to gage them for what they were worth and class them along with the froth on a soda or the sputter of a freshly lighted match. The thing underneath was what mattered and he knew well that beneath the torrent of words his mother was the best mother on earth, so what more could a boy ask?

Therefore he stood before her, whistling softly and waiting to see what would happen next. For something surely would happen; it always did when Mrs. McGregor rolled up her sleeves, and they were rolled up now, displaying beneath the margin of blue gingham a powerful arm terminating in a strong hand and slender, capable fingers.

Years ago she had come to Mulberry Court with a large brood of children and it had been a long time before she could number one friend among her neighbors. The chief complaint entered against her was that she was not sociable, and if you were not sociable at Mulberry Court it meant you were lofty, uppish, considered yourself better than other folks. What it really meant, however, was that you did not hang out of your window and chatter to the inhabitant of the opposite tenement; or loiter in the doorway or on the sidewalk to gossip with the women who lived on the floors below.

At the outset Mrs. McGregor had let it be understood that she had no time for gossip and it was this decree that had earned for her the stigma of not being sociable, the acme of all crimes at Mulberry Court. Of course she had not proclaimed her policy in so many words. No, indeed! Yet she might as well have done so for the business-like manner in which she hastened home from market and shot up the stairs published her philosophy more forcefully than any words could have done.

"She's just too good for the rest of us," announced Mrs. O'Dowd sarcastically to the little circle who were wont to await her verdict on every newcomer to the district. "Proud and snappy and stuck-up, I call her. Not much of an addition to the house, if you ask my opinion."

This snapshot judgment, hasty as it was, was promptly accepted by the other women, for was not Julie O'Dowd the social dictator of the community? Had she ever been known to be wrong? With one accord Mulberry Court turned its back on the new arrival who so flagrantly defied the etiquette of the place.

Indeed had not Mrs. O'Dowd's baby fallen ill the seal of disapproval put on Mrs. McGregor might have rested on her all her days, and she and her entire family been completely ostracized by the neighborhood. But little Joey O'Dowd, the youngest of Julie's flock, was seized with pneumonia, and although the flock was a large one Julie was too genuine a mother to feel she could spare one out of her fold. Was not Joey the littlest of all, the pet of her household? All the motherhood in her revolted at the thought of losing him. Strangely enough until the present moment she had escaped great crises with her children. She was well schooled in the ways of whooping cough, measles, and chicken pox and could do up a cut finger with almost professional skill; but in the face of crucial illness she was like a warrior without weapons.

Overwhelmed with terror, therefore, by the immediate calamity, she did in benumbed fashion everything the doctor directed and still Joey was no better; if anything he grew steadily worse. Motionless he lay in his crib, his great staring eyes giving forth no flicker of recognition. There was not much hope, the neighbors whispered, after they had tiptoed in to look at him and tiptoed out again. He was as good as gone. Julie could never save him in the world.

The whispers, humanely muffled, did not reach the panic-stricken mother but she was not blind to the despairing head-shaking and these suddenly awakened her to the realization that according to general opinion the battle she was waging was a losing one. It was a terrible discovery. What should she do? She must do something. Wild-eyed she plunged into the hall, a vague impulse to seek help moving her; and it was just as she paused irresolute at the head of the stairs that she came face to face with Mrs. McGregor ascending to her fifth-floor flat.

Now Mrs. McGregor was a born nurse, whose skill had been increased by constant practice. With a wisdom that amounted almost to genius she had brought her large family through many an appalling conflict and emerged victorious. Sickness, therefore, had no terrors for her. Instantly the mother in her read and interpreted the desperation in Julie's face and without a word she slipped through the open door into the room where Joey lay. One glance of her experienced eye showed that there was plenty to be done. The interior was close and untidy, for Mrs. O'Dowd in her distraction had cast aside every consideration but her baby.

Mrs. McGregor stooped down over the crib.

What she saw there or did not see she at least kept to herself, and when she straightened up it was to meet the searching gaze of her neighbor with a grave smile.

"He's going to die," moaned Julie, wringing her hands. "He is going to die—my baby—and I can't help it!"

Although for a long time the two women had lived beneath the same roof, these were the first words Mrs. O'Dowd had ever addressed to Mrs. McGregor.

"Might I touch him?" the latter inquired gently.

Like a suspicious animal Julie stiffened jealously.

"I'll not hurt him," Mrs. McGregor hastened to say, not taking offense at the other's attitude. "I just want to raise him up so he can breathe better." Then she added reassuringly, "I'd not give up if I were you. You must keep on fighting to the very last minute. There is much we can do yet to make him comfortable."

"What?"

"We can bathe him a little for one thing, if you would heat some water."

Dumbly Julie turned to obey.

"I've a big family of my own," went on Mrs. McGregor in matter-of-fact fashion, "and I've seen so many children pull through when they looked fit to die that I've learned never to quit hoping. You'll get nowhere in a fight if you haven't courage."

"I had courage enough at first," whispered the baby's mother in a shaking voice, "but I've lost my nerve now. I'm frightened— and—and tired."

Tears came into her eyes.

"Of course you are," came with quick sympathy from Mrs. McGregor. "We all are apt to lose our nerve when we are worn out. I don't wonder you're tired. You've had no sleep day or night, I'll be bound."

"Not much. The neighbors were kind about offering but somehow I couldn't leave Joey with 'em. Besides, how can you sleep when you are worried half out of your mind?"

"I know! I know!" nodded the other woman. "Still you can't go on forever without rest. Next you know you will be down sick yourself and then where will your baby be—to say nothing of your other children. A mother has got to think ahead. Now listen. Would you trust me to watch the baby while you curled up on the sofa and got a wink or two of sleep? I'll promise to call you should there be an atom of change. Do now! Be a sensible woman. And how would you feel about my giving the little chap a drop of medicine? A Scotch doctor in the old country once gave me a prescription that I've tried on both Timmie and Martin and it did 'em worlds of good at a time just like this. It might do nothing for your child, mind. I'm not promising it would. Still, it couldn't hurt him and it might cure."

Julie's dulled mind caught the final word. *Cure!* Alas, she had given up hope that anything in the world could do that. The reaction that came with the suggestion was so wonderful that it left her speechless.

"Now see here," burst out Mrs. McGregor misinterpreting her silence, "use your common sense. Do I look as if I had come to poison your baby? Why, woman, I love children better than anything on earth. They're a precious lot of bother, there's no denying, and sometimes I get that impatient with one or the other of 'em I could toss him out the window. But for all their hectoring, and their noise, and their dirt—their meddling, and smashing, and mending, I'd not be without them."

While speaking she had been touching the baby with a hand so yearning and tender that it could not be stayed. She had raised his head, smoothed his pillow, straightened the coverings that lay over him. It was amazing how quietly and deftly her hands moved. Even the child seemed conscious of her healing presence, for all of a sudden his wee fingers curled about one of hers and he smiled faintly.

"See!" exclaimed Mrs. McGregor, "the baby is not afraid to trust me."

"Nor am I any longer," put in Julie with eager surrender. "Do as you like with Joey. You know better than I."

"Oh, it isn't that," the visitor protested, rising. "It is just that it's sometimes well not to leave a stone unturned. You might regret not having taken the chance. I'll slip upstairs and get the medicine. It won't take a minute."

"If you'll be that kind."

The Scotchwoman needed no second bidding. She was gone and back again in a twinkling, the magic green bottle in her hand.

"Now if I might have a cup of hot water," said she. "I've a dropper here. We'll see what a spoonful of this mixture will do for the wee laddie. What is his name?"

"Joey."

Mrs. O'Dowd's eyes had brightened and they now beamed on her neighbor.

"It's a nice name," replied Mrs. McGregor, beaming in turn. "I always liked the name of Joseph. Well, Joey boy, we'll see if we can make you well. Here, little fellow!"

Gently she forced the liquid between the baby's lips.

"Now we'll sponge him a bit, put on a fresh slip, and give him some air!"

"But won't he——"

"Catch cold? Not if he is shielded from the draught. He'll like the air and feel the better for it. It will help him to breathe."

Noiselessly she went to work and within an hour both Joey and his surroundings took on a different aspect.

"Now," said she to the grateful mother, "you roll up in that comforter and take a nap. Don't worry about the baby. I'll be right here. Will you trust me?"

Julie hesitated.

"It's not that I won't trust you," murmured she. "But you're so heavenly kind. Not another soul has done for me what you have and I'm a hundred times better acquainted with 'em, too. Of course I know they have all they can do without taking on the cares of others. I'm not blaming them. You yourself can't have much time to spare. Haven't you other things to do?"

"Of course I have," came with curt honesty from Mrs.

McGregor. "I've six children and they leave me little time for idling. But when I do take time away from 'em, I plan to take it to some purpose. Just now I have nothing more important to do than nurse this baby. It's my first job. So don't be worrying about my work. Luckily it is Saturday and Mary, Carl, and Timmie will look after the little tots and get the dinner. I told 'em to when I was there just now. Martin and Nell seldom give any trouble, and should James Frederick wake up, one of the boys is to run down and tell me."

Julie placed a hand impulsively on that of the other woman.

"I can never thank you," murmured she brokenly.

"Oh, don't be talking of thanks," Mrs. McGregor interrupted, cutting her short. "My dosing may do no good and before the day is out you may be calling me a meddlesome old harridan. Wait and see what happens. I'm not one that sets much store by thanks, anyhow. After all, what does it amount to but a string of words? If we can cure the baby it will be all the thanks I want."

If the sentiment the final phrase so modestly expressed was genuine Mrs. McGregor at least received the boon she craved, for as if by magic the baby began to mend that very night and before the week passed was out of danger and on the high road to recovery. Julie's gratitude was touching to see.

"'Twas Mrs. McGregor saved Joey," declared she to every person she met. "She's as good as any doctor—better, for Joey might have died but for her. Should I go through life kneeling to her on my bended knees I never could thank her enough."

Julie O'Dowd did not go through life, however, kneeling before Mrs. McGregor on her bended knees; but she did a more practical and efficacious thing. Everywhere she went she sounded the praise of her neighbor; talked of her kindness, her wisdom, her unselfishness, until not only Mulberry Court, but the area adjoining it began to view the gaunt, austere figure from quite a different angle. Shyly the women began to nod a greeting to the stranger.

"It's just her way to be curt and quick," explained they to one another. "She doesn't mean a thing in the world by it. Julie says she's sharp and prickly as a chestnut burr, but with the sweetest of hearts inside."

Indeed it was not long before Mrs. McGregor proved her right to this generous summary of her character. Other neighbors gained courage to consult her about their children and in time about their troubles in general.

"Ask Mrs. McGregor," became the slogan of Mulberry Court. "She'll know."

And she unfailingly did. She it was who prescribed medicines; gave advice; suggested plain, common-sense remedies for every variety of dilemma. Nevertheless she wasted no words about it. She had no time to fool away, she let it be known. Whatever she did had to be done with pitiless directness. Often her council was delivered through a crack in the door or even given through the door itself; and there were instances when it was shouted through the keyhole. But no matter where the words came from they were always helpful and friendly and the neighbors came to understand the manner accompanying them and did not resent it.

Her children understood it too. Mary, Carl, Timmie, Martin, four-year-old Nell, and even wee James Frederick (whom Mrs. McGregor unfailingly addressed by his full name) all understood and worshipped their quick-tongued mother. Together with the rest of Mulberry Court they also had supreme faith in whatever she did and said, and were certain that every calamity under the sun could be set right if only she were consulted and her advice followed.

And yet loyal as they were, there was one point on which neither Carl nor Mary agreed with their mother. Of course she was right—she must be right; wasn't she always so? Yet notwithstanding this belief they could not but feel that it would be a far better arrangement for them to leave school and go into the cotton mills where their father had worked for so many years. Ever so many of the boys and girls they knew worked there. Why should they remain in the High School struggling with algebra, geometry, history, Latin, English and bookkeeping when they might be earning money? It seemed senseless. Certainly the family needed money badly enough. Were there not always endless pairs of shoes to be bought? Caps, mittens, suits, stockings, and underclothing to purchase; not to mention food and groceries? And then there was the rent.

Ah, Mary and Carl knew very well about the rent, the bills, and all the other worrisome things. Even Timmie, who was only nine, knew about them; and once Martin, aged six, had startled his elders by proclaiming on a sunny May morning, "This is rent day, isn't it, Ma?" in a tone of awe, as if the date marked some gruesome ceremony.

You came to understand about rent day when toward the end of the month there were no pennies to be had, and you were forced to wait for the shoes or rubbers you needed.

That rent day was a milestone to be dreaded even Nell vaguely guessed and when it had passed in safety all the McGregors, both big and little, joined in a general rejoicing.

Ma was the magician who accomplished that happy miracle. Ma always contrived to accomplish everything, so of course she managed rent day along with the rest of the wonders she performed. She made no secret, either, of how she did it. She sewed! Yes, she sewed for a dressmaker who sent her marvelous dresses to embroider. For Ma was very clever with her needle and right out of the blue sky could make the most beautiful flowers and figures with colored silks. She could also do beading and she was teaching Mary how to do it. Already Mary could do quite nice embroidery and exquisite plain sewing.

Ma was very proud of this.

But what Mary did chiefly when she was not at school was to help with the housework so her mother would be free to sew. That was the important thing. Ma must not roughen her hands or the silks she worked with would be spoiled. So Mary cooked and scrubbed like a real little housewife; took care of the younger children and kept them quiet so they would not interrupt their mother.

And between school hours Carl and Tim helped also. They built the fires, wiped the dishes, ran errands, and brought home any bits of discarded wood they found in the streets. In fact, there was not one drone in the McGregor hive. Even James Frederick had learned to lie in his crib and play by himself when everybody was busy.

It was a happy family, the McGregors. Its members, it is true, did not have everything they wanted. They never expected that. Those who had mittens lacked new caps, and those who had caps were often forced to wear patched shoes and made-over stockings. Martin's reefer frequently did duty for Nell, and Mrs. McGregor's cape for Mary. However, all that did not matter. They were happy and that was the chief thing, happy in spite of patched clothing, coats that were outgrown, rubbers that were either sizes too small or dropped off at every step, and shoes that were common property. The little flat was sometimes hot in summer and cold in winter but it took more than that to dampen the McGregors' spirits.

When they had lentil soup, how steaming and delicious it was! When meat stew, what a dish for the gods! And who could have asked for a greater treat than a thick slice of Mary's fresh bread coated over with molasses or peanut butter?

Every month a long blue envelope containing a check from Uncle Frederick arrived and that, together with what Mary and her mother earned, kept the household going. But they seldom saw Uncle James Frederick Dillingham. He was always sailing to India, China, or South America. Sometimes letters came from him and picture postcards showing strange countries and people in foreign dress. But the check never failed to make its appearance and as it was highly important that it should, everybody agreed that since Uncle Frederick could not come himself he was almost as satisfactorily represented by this magic bit of blue paper. The check brought things and perhaps if Uncle Frederick himself had come he wouldn't. You could not tell about uncles you had never seen.

In the meantime the blue paper kept stew in the kettle and the shelter of Mulberry Court above their heads, and what better service could an uncle render his relatives?

Hence Uncle Frederick's name came to be mentioned constantly in the household.

"Remember, Timmie, those are your Uncle Frederick Dillingham's rubber boots and be thankful to him for them," the boy's mother would observe when she brought home the purchase. Or "Uncle Frederick is presenting you with those stockings, Carl. See you don't forget it."

And the children did not forget. Gradually their unknown uncle came to assume in their imagination a form that would have surprised him had he been suddenly confronted by it. It was that of a benevolent-faced fairy clad in robes of purple and ermine, and wearing on his head a crown resplendent with gems of myriad colors. In his hand he carried a scepter terminating in a star that far outshone the jewels he wore, a scepter all powerful to work miracles. He was the good angel of the McGregor home, the Aladdin to whom they owed all sorts of blessings.

And yet withal Uncle James Frederick Dillingham was one and the same person who sailed the *Charlotte* to India, China, South America, or some other ephemeral port. How paradoxical was this dual rôle, how alluring and how ridiculous!

CARL TELLS A STORY

It was April. Already spring was in the air. The grass in the parks was turning green, forsythia bloomed golden, and boys were playing marbles on the streets and sidewalks. Even Mulberry Court, shut in as it was, felt the impulse of the awakening season. The landlord came, looked over the premises, and after viewing the general shabbiness became reckless enough to order a broken windowpane to be reset, some of the tumble-down ceilings to be repaired, and the fire escapes and window frames to be repainted.

Painting at Mulberry Court was a terrible ordeal. As there was not an inch of the place that was not crowded to the limit of its capacity, painting meant that milk bottles, improvised ice chests, and woodpiles must be put somewhere else; and where that somewhere could be was an enigma. Furthermore, to add to this difficulty there were the children—dozens of them tumbling over one another and surging in and out the doors, a fact that rendered painting a precarious undertaking. Youthful investigators examined the moist pigment; chubby fingers drew hieroglyphics in it; while the less curious forgot it altogether and carried away on their garments imprints of vermilion and black that transformed their otherwise dingy garments into robes of oriental splendor.

Carl McGregor was no exception to the rule for wherever calamity lurked he was sure to be in its vicinity.

"I'd know you'd never rest until you got a patch of red paint on yourself," announced his mother, surveying him as he started toward the door. "As, if buying you sweaters ain't enough without your leaning plumb up against the fire escape and stamping a whole decalcomania of red stripes on your back like as if you were a convict."

"Is there paint on me, Ma?"

"Is there? I suppose you had no notion of it."

"I hadn't—honest Injun."

"Well, aside from the fact that you're barred up and down neat as if the lines were ruled there's nothing the matter with you," returned his mother with a faint smile.

"Oh, I'm awfully sorry, Ma. Truly I am."

"Sorry? I'll be bound you are. You are always a bundle of regrets when it is too late to help anything. However, you need weep no tears for that sweater needed washing anyway. You're that rough on your clothes that none of 'em keep clean more than a minute. I'll get some gasoline and soak it out in the shed and it will be like new. Peel it off and give it to me."

"I'm sorry, Ma," the boy repeated.

"It's no great matter, sonny. Children must be children. I'm past expecting them to be grown-ups," his mother said kindly. "If you hadn't been getting into the paint you most likely would have been getting into something else. You have a genius for such mishaps. I'm glad it was no worse."

Reassured, Carl grinned.

"I do seem to have a good many—" he hesitated, then added, "misfortunes."

"Misfortunes, do you call 'em? Sure that's a pretty polite

word to apply to the things that manage to happen to you," sniffed Mrs. McGregor. "I suppose it was a misfortune when you tumbled underneath the watering cart; and a misfortune when you sat down in the wet tar! A misfortune when you sent the snowball through the schoolroom window; to say nothing of the creamcake you treated Jakie Sullivan to that well-nigh killed him."

"I didn't know the creamcake was going to make him sick."

"No; 'twas just your misfortune. You seem to attract adventures like that. Why, if I was to let you go into the cotton mills as you are always begging to do you'd have every machine there out of order in less than a week and yourself hashed up into little pieces into the bargain."

She had touched upon an unlucky subject for instantly, with flaming face, the lad confronted her.

"No, I wouldn't. I wish you would let me go into the mills, Ma. You might let me try it. Ever so many boys no older than I are working there and earning oodles of money. If we had more money we could——"

"We could be having an automobile, no doubt, and going to Palm Beach winters," was the grim response. "Well, Palm Beach or not, you're not going into any mill so long as we can keep body and soul together without your doing it. You are going to get an education—you and Mary too—if it costs me my life. I'm not going to have you grow up knowing nothing and being nothing. Some day you'll see I was right and thank me for it."

"I thank you now, Ma," declared Carl soberly. "But that doesn't make me relish Latin and history any better."

"No matter if it doesn't. What you like is of no consequence," Mrs. McGregor announced, with a majestic sweep of her hand. "The chief thing is that you exercise your mind and learn how to use it. The Latin itself amounts to nothing. It is like boxing gloves or a punching bag, a thing that serves its turn to limber up your brain. It is learning to think that counts."

Carl's face brightened.

"The teacher was saying something like that just the other day," asserted he eagerly. "He was telling us about some of the people who had done great things in the world and explaining how long and how hard they had to work at them. The inventors, for instance, had to think and think about the things they invented. It didn't just come to them all in a minute as I used to believe it did."

Although his mother did not look up from her sewing she nodded encouragingly.

"There was Eli Whitney," continued Carl, coming nearer. "I remembered about him because of the mills here. He invented the cotton gin, you know. Mr. Kimball told us that Whitney went through Yale and then started down South to be a tutor in somebody's family without any idea of ever being an inventor. But when he got to where he was going the people who had hired him had changed their minds and found somebody else and poor Eli Whitney was out of a job."

"A shabby trick!"

"Yes. Still, it was lucky for him, just the same," responded Carl, "because on the way down he had met the widow of General Greene and she was sorry for him and asked him to her house. He'd just been vaccinated because there was lots of smallpox in the South and he was feeling rotten. You know how sore your arm gets and how sick you are sometimes. Remember Martin? Well, anyhow, Mrs. Greene either knew what it meant to be vaccinated or else she was kind of ashamed of the way her part of the country had treated Eli Whitney. Or maybe she was just kind-hearted like you. Anyhow she invited Mr. Whitney to come to Savannah when she saw how mean he felt and the fit he threw at finding himself so far from home without money or a job."

"Carl!"

"Well, wouldn't you have thrown a fit? I think Mrs. Greene was a peach," went on Carl, passing serenely over the reproof. "She was mighty kind to take a stranger into her house when he had no friends."

"Certainly."

"By this time Mr. Whitney had decided to be a lawyer and while he was making his home at Mrs. Greene's he began to read all the law books he could lay hands on. Then one day Mrs. Greene busted her embroidery frame——"

"Did *what*?"

"Oh, you know, Ma," fretted Carl, at being interrupted. "She smashed the thing and——"

"What had that to do with it?"

"Everything; because, you see, Eli Whitney mended it so nicely that Mrs. Greene was pleased into the ground and thought he was the smartest person ever. His father had had a shop at home where as a boy he had learned to use tools. But of course Mrs. Greene didn't know that. All she knew was that he made a corking job of her embroidery frame and so one day when some Georgia gentlemen were there at dinner and were telling how hard it was to get the seeds out of cotton she up and said, 'You should ask Mr. Whitney how to do it; he can do anything,' and to prove it she toted out her embroidery frame to show them."

"Did *what*?"

"Oh, say, Ma, don't keep bothering me when I'm trying to

tell you a story," Carl complained peevishly. "You know what I mean well enough."

"Much as ever," was the grim reply.

The lad grinned.

"Well, anyhow, the Georgia cotton men talked to Eli Whitney, explaining how the cotton stuck to the seeds and got all broken to bits when you tried to get them out; and how it took nearly a whole day to separate a pound of cotton fiber from the seeds. And then the cotton planters went on to tell how there was lots and lots of land in the South where you couldn't raise rice but could raise cotton if it wasn't such a chore—" (a warning glance from his mother caused Carl hastily to amend the phrase) "such a piece of work to get the seeds out. Eli Whitney listened to their talk and after the men had gone he thought he'd try to make some sort of a machine that would clear cotton of the seeds."

"And did he?"

"You betcha! I mean, yes, he did. Whitney was no boob." (This time Mrs. McGregor failed to protest; perhaps she decided it was useless.) "He had, as I told you, made wheels and canes and knives and nails in his father's workshop at home. He had even made a violin. So he wasn't at all fussed about trying to make a cotton gin. I guess he had a hunch he could do it."

"A *what?*" gasped Mrs. McGregor involuntarily.

"A hunch means he knew he could turn the trick."

The mother shook her head ruefully.

"And me almost killing myself to give you an education!" she ejaculated beneath her breath.

"Well, anyway, Ma, slang or no slang, I'd be telling you nothing at all about Eli Whitney if I hadn't gone to school, so cheer up," asserted Carl impishly.

He heard his mother laugh. Mrs. McGregor had the good old Scotch sense of humor and when her flashing smile came it was always a delight to the beholder.

"You're a good boy, Carl, if you do speak the language of an orang-outang," she answered. "Where you pick up such a dialect I cannot imagine."

"Oh, it's easy enough to pick it up, Ma. The stunt is not to. Why, what I've been saying just now is nothing to what I could say if I let myself go. I've been holding in because of you. I could have had you so locoed you couldn't have understood a thing I meant if I hadn't been—been considerate. But I know you don't like slang so I try to cut it out. You may not believe it but I do try—honest, I do."

"I believe you, laddie," returned his mother kindly. "It's hard, I know, with all the other boys talking like barbarians. Now go on about Mr. Whitney. Did he contrive to make the machine the Georgia gentlemen wanted?"

"Yes, siree!" continued Carl with enthusiasm. "Mrs. Greene gave him a room to work in down in the basement of her house and he set right about the job. Unluckily he had never seen any cotton growing because he had always lived in the North, you know. In fact, he had never laid eyes on cotton at all until it was made into cloth, so of course he hadn't much of an idea what he was up against, and the first thing he had to do was to scurry round and get specimens of cotton with the seeds in it. It wasn't so easy to do just then, either, because it was not the season for cotton-gathering and he had to hunt and hunt to get some of the last season's crop. I believe he finally got what he needed from a warehouse in New Orleans. Anyhow, he got the cotton pods somewhere and found out better where he stood. And that reminds me, Ma, that the teacher told us there were ever so many different kinds of cotton; and that the Upland cotton, growing in the South, had green seeds that stuck like—like *anything* to the white part. You could hardly separate the two without ruining the cotton fibers and you can see that as they were to be spun they must not be broken."

"Mr. Whitney did have a puzzle to work out."

"You've said it, Ma! He sure had," beamed Carl. "Well, he kept fussing round, and fussing round, and by and by he managed to get together a simple sort of contrivance that would do what he wanted it to. It was no great shakes of a machine. Any blacksmith or wheelwright could have made it if he had happened to think of it first. In fact, lots of other people did make gins like it. That is why Whitney never got rich, the teacher said."

"But didn't he get his invention patented?" inquired Mrs. McGregor, laying aside the tulle she was beading.

"Not until it was too late. You see, Mrs. Greene was so set up to think Mr. Whitney had done the deed she had predicted he would that she had to go blabbing all over town how clever he was. And the minute people heard that a cotton gin was really made that would take out the seeds they came begging to see the wonderful machine and find out how it worked; and of course Mr. Whitney had to show it off. He hadn't a notion people would be so low-down as to snitch his idea and go to making cotton gins of their own. But that's exactly what they did do and as soon as Mr. Whitney and Mr. Miller who was helping him got wise to the fact, they locked the new cotton gin up. But do you s'pose that did any good? Not on your life! The cotton raisers were crazy to get the machine because everybody needed it so badly. On the plantations there wasn't enough work to keep the negro slaves busy and it cost a lot to feed them. The planters figured that if something profitable could be found for them to do they would earn their keep. They certainly could not do this picking the seeds out of cotton because it took them such an age to pick enough to make a pound. They could gather the crop all right. It had to be gathered by hand. What was needed was something that would take the seeds out and make it possible to raise and sell big quantities of cotton. So Whitney's gin exactly filled the bill. It was just what the whole South had been waiting for and if such a thing existed people were bound to have it. Naturally when Whitney wouldn't show it to them and locked it up, they thought he was almighty stingy and some of the meanest of the bunch broke into the place where he kept it and carried it off."

"Oh!"

"Rotten, wasn't it? They ought to have been hung; but they weren't. Instead, the model of the cotton gin got abroad and all the South started to making cotton gins until they were all over the place."

"I'm afraid Mr. Whitney wasn't a very business-like man," ventured Mrs. McGregor.

"He wasn't. Most generally inventors aren't, I guess. Still, how was he to know they were going to swipe his idea? Of course he and Mr. Miller went straight to work and tried to pick up the pieces. Mr. Whitney went home to New Haven and set about making cotton gins on a larger scale than he could make them at Mrs. Greene's; but even then he could not make them fast enough. And on top of all his factory burned down and for a while he couldn't make any gins at all. It seemed as if hard luck pursued him whichever way he turned."

"It certainly did seem so!"

"He and Mr. Miller, who had now gone in as his partner, spent no end of money in lawsuits, and Mr. Miller got so worn out and discouraged fighting the infringers that finally he died, leaving

Eli Whitney to carry on the battle alone. And it was a battle, too, to get any satisfaction out of the people who were making use of his idea. I believe that North Carolina and Tennessee did pay him something, and after a while South Carolina and Georgia did. In all he received about ninety thousand dollars; but the lawsuits he had been compelled to go through to get it ate up a good slice of the receipts. Besides, some more had to go for the factory that got burned and other expenses. So he didn't get much out of the deal, I guess. But the South did. The Whitney gin whooped up their cotton trade in great style. Every year the planters grew more and more cotton because now that they could get the seeds out it paid to raise it, and by and by they were exporting millions of bales. Cotton is now one of our biggest exports, the teacher said. We grow billions of pounds of it and for the most part it is the green seed, Upland cotton, cleaned by a gin founded on Whitney's idea. That's why I say it does you no good to go to school," concluded Carl. "Whitney went through Yale college and invented his cotton gin before he had been out of the university a year, and what good did it do him, I'd like to know?"

"He did a lot to help the world along, sonny."

"Oh, I suppose he did," admitted the boy. "But for all that he didn't get the spondulics. That is why I want to go into the factory. So I can get some cash to help out here at home. S'pos'n we didn't have Uncle Frederick Dillingham or your sewing money? And anyhow, I don't want you to be always sewing. I want you to have pretty clothes, ride round in an automobile, and be a lady!"

"Oh, Carlie! Can't one work for a living and still be a lady, my dear?"

Carl flushed.

"Of course she can, Ma. You're a lady right now. Still, I do wish you didn't have to make those silly dresses all the time.

Well, no matter. You just wait until I get through school. You shall be wearing dresses like those and somebody else shall be sewing the beads on."

A suspicious moisture gathered in Mrs. McGregor's eyes.

"You're a good boy, Carl," answered she gently, "even if you do slaughter your mother tongue. Now be off with you. All this palaver about Mr. Whitney has almost made you late for school, and left me hardly knowing whether I am sewing frontwards or backwards. Still, it isn't a bad thing to have a son that knows something."

It was evident from Mrs. McGregor's tone that she might have said more but for the stern belief that she must not flatter her children. Therefore to cut short the danger of such a crime she brusquely hurried Carl out of the kitchen, merely calling after him:

"Don't forget to bring home a yeast cake to-night or you'll get no bread to-morrow. Put your mind on it, now. If you remembered the errands I ask you to do half as well as you remember about cotton gins and the like you'd save layers of shoe leather."

It was a characteristic farewell. Mrs. McGregor would not have been Mrs. McGregor had she not uttered it. All this Carl understood and, undaunted by the words, he bent to kiss his mother on the cheek.

"I suppose you wouldn't have time to stop into the Harlings on your way," suggested she, with a twinkle in her eye.

"I was planning to stop there a minute as I went along."

"I'll be bound you were. One might as well try to keep a fly out of the molasses as to keep you away from the Harlings. Well, since you are going that way anyhow, you can carry over a bowl of broth. I made it yesterday a-purpose. Tell Mrs. Harling it will only need to be heated up for herself and Grandfather Harling."

CHAPTER III

A TRAGEDY

It was in the corner block beyond Mulberry Court that the Harlings lived, and had you asked Carl McGregor or his chum Jack Sullivan who Hal Harling was you would have received in return for your ignorance a withering stare, a sigh of pity, or possibly no reply at all. Any one who did not know Hal Harling was either to be scorned or condoled with, as the case might be. Yet each boy would have found it difficult to put into words who and what this distinguished personage really was.

Hal Harling was the embryo political boss of the district; the leader of the gang; the hero of every boy who lived within a radius of half a mile of the dingy flat on Broad Street. He was a tall, jovial-faced, thick-set fellow with the physique of a prize fighter and such an abundance of careless good humor that it bubbled contagiously from his round blue eyes and smiling lips. One would have said he was the last person in the world to take offence and indeed on first glance one might safely have made the assertion. But with this gay, happy-go-lucky disposition went a highly developed desire for fair play which at times suddenly converted the balmy, easy-going young autocrat into an enemy pitiless and terrible.

Let some brute stone a kitten; torment a boy smaller than

himself; snatch an apple from the stall of the old woman at the corner and, with a justice whose speed was incredible, Hal Harding descended upon the miscreant and pommeled into him a lesson in squareness that he did not soon forget.

The fact that the youthful avenger was usually on the right side increased, if anything, the number of street brawls he was mixed up in, for alas, Mulberry Court and all the outlying vicinity teemed with so great a multitude of injustices that he who set himself to straighten them out found ample provocation for continual blows. As he trod the narrow streets and alleys this champion of the weak encountered one challenge after another with the result that it was a common sight in the neighborhood to see Hal Harling the center of an angry scuffle.

Partisanship was instant. A passer-by did not need to investigate the broil. Ten cases out of eleven the victim of the squabble was getting what was coming to him, in popular opinion.

"Hal Harling was giving it to him good and plenty," a sympathetic observer would afterward relate. "I don't know what the fuss was about but I didn't interfere for I'll wager Hal was right; he usually is."

Around the standard of such a personality it was inevitable that the inhabitants of the community, especially the male ones, should rally; and foremost in the ranks of admiring worshippers were Jack Sullivan and Carl McGregor, either one of whom would willingly have rolled up his own sleeves in defense of his idol. They tagged at his heels, ran his errands, and walked on air whenever they won his commendation. If he called them down it was as if they had been rolled in the dust.

And yet despite the incense burned at his shrine Hal Harling kept a level head and an estimate of himself that was appealingly modest. In fact he was a very human boy with the same love of pranks and mischief that delighted other boys. He loved a joke dearly. It was fun, for example, to let an orange down on a string and dangle it before little Katie Callahan's window and then jerk it back out of Katie's reach when she snatched for it. Or it amused him to drop peppermint balls through the Murphy's letter box and hear the children inside the room chase them as they rolled about the floor. Later he saw to it that Katie got the orange and the Murphy youngsters the candy. All his jokes were like that, their playful hectoring ending in kindness. He was too kind-hearted to enjoy causing pain.

What wonder that such a hero had his satellites?

On the other hand, he had his enemies too—scores of them—for a justice dealer is never without opponents. As a rule these persons were the victims of his various avalanches of wrath, those to whom at one time or another he had meted out punishment and denounced as cowards. For the disapproval of these cravens Hal Harling did not care a button. He much preferred they should be numbered among his enemies rather than his friends and he said so frankly. Nevertheless, his mother, timid by nature and of a peace-loving disposition, shook her head.

"You can't afford, Hal, to antagonize folks the way you do," she would protest. "The time may come when you'll be sorry."

For answer the giant would shrug his shoulders.

"I'm not afraid of anybody," he would reply proudly.

The statement was not made in a spirit of bravado; rather it reflected the self-respect of one consciously in the right.

"But you need to be more careful. Such people are capable of working you harm."

"Let them try."

"But they are. They can do all sorts of underhanded things

you would not descend to," whimpered Mrs. Harling. "It worries me all the time to see you so regardless."

"There, there, Mother! Quit fussing about me," pleaded the big fellow kindly. "I'm all right and can look after myself."

"I know you can when the fight is a fair one," agreed his mother. "But you never can tell what weapon a coward will use."

Hal laughed contemptuously and, realizing that her counsel had failed of its aim, Mrs. Harling said no more.

Up to the present the calamities she periodically predicted had not occurred and as those who loved her son rallied round him with ever-increasing loyalty, and those who disliked him kept their distance, she gradually ceased to protest. What was the use of wasting her strength on conditions she could not help? Poor soul! She needed every atom of energy she possessed to meet the trials that beset her own path.

For Mrs. Harling was a helpless invalid and together with her bedridden father lived day after day imprisoned in the small tenement overlooking the rushing, hurrying world of which she was no part. Each morning Louise, Hal's younger sister, made tidy the house, packed up a luncheon, and the two started for Davis and Coulter's spinning mills where all day they helped to operate the busy machinery. It was a noisy, monotonous occupation; a stretch of dull, wearisome hours, and frequently the boy and girl were so tired at night they had scarcely energy to move. And yet they toiled at the humdrum task gratefully, rejoicing in their wages which not only kept body and soul together but provided for the feeble mother and the aged grandfather.

The past winter had been a hard one in Baileyville, the manufacturing village where they lived. Most of the mills were running on half time and many of the employés had been turned away for lack of work. In consequence worry and uncertainty hung over everybody. Who would be the next to go, they speculated. One never could predict where the axe would fall, or be sure he might not be the victim elected to meet its merciless stroke.

Thus far both Hal and Louise had been retained at their posts; but the fear that some of the older operatives who had been longer in the employ of the company might take precedence over them constantly menaced their peace of mind.

Corcoran, the foreman under whom they worked, was a harsh, unreasonable bully who rather enjoyed his post as executioner, authority having exaggerated in him all the meannesses that lurked in his small, vindictive nature. Only the week before, Hal, enraged by his discourtesy and injustice to one of the women, had blurted out to his face a rebuke for his roughness. It was, to be sure, an unwise act and one that not only did the poor girl whose cause he championed little good but jeopardized his own position; yet to save his soul he could not have checked his indignation.

"You shouldn't have said it," declared Louise, who had been an eyewitness of the encounter. "Of course I was proud of you as could be; and you said nothing but what Corcoran deserved. Still it isn't safe to do that sort of thing. It may lose you your job."

"I don't care if it does," returned Hal, whose rage had not yet cooled. "Corcoran may fire me if he wants to. But he isn't going to bully any girl as he bullied Susie Mayo—not when I'm round."

"But don't you see, dear; we can't afford to lose our jobs," continued his sister gently. "Too much depends on our keeping them. We must have the money."

"I'm not worrying," laughed Hal with confidence. "If Corcoran should give me the sack I could get another place without any trouble, I'll bet I could."

"Places are not so easy to find," asserted the more prudent Louise. "There are lots of men in Baileyville who have been out of work for months. You ought not to be in such a hurry to rush into a quarrel, Hal."

"I was right; you say so yourself."

"Yes, perhaps so. Still——"

"Don't you think somebody ought to have called Corcoran down?"

"Of course he was unfair and—and rude."

"Rude!" interrupted her brother scornfully, "he was contemptible, outrageous!"

"I know it. But——"

"If fewer people stood for brutes there would be fewer brutes in the world."

"It isn't our business to round Corcoran up."

"It is my business to stop any man who is impolite to a woman," replied Hal. "Besides, Corcoran knew well enough he was wrong. You notice he did not put up any defense. He just walked off and has never mentioned the affair since."

"That is what frightens me."

"What do you mean?"

"I'm afraid he isn't through."

"Nonsense! He's through all right. He hasn't uttered a yip and it is now over two weeks ago that the thing happened. Quit your worrying, kiddie. There'll be no comeback from Corcoran."

The reassuring words, so confidently spoken, did much to allay Louise's fears. Uneventfully the days slipped by, and with every one that passed the boy and girl breathed more freely. Not only were they skilled workers but they were earnest and ambitious to give of their best. Moreover they had behind them an untarnished record for faithful attendance at the mills. Such service, argued they, must be of value, and when matched against much of the grudging, incompetent labor about them should be of sufficient worth to keep them on Davis and Coulter's payroll. All they asked was fair play and to be judged on their merits. This demand seemed reasonable enough; but alas, the world is not always a just dealer and when on a Saturday morning not long before Christmas Louise Harling looked into her pay envelope a cry of dismay escaped her.

The fate she had feared had overtaken her. Davis and Coulter informed her that after the fifteenth of the month, which fell a week hence, the firm would not need her services.

Instantly two thoughts rushed to her mind. One was whether Hal had also received similar notice; and the other was that all the holiday plans she had so fondly cherished must now go by the boards. She would have no money to buy presents or a Christmas dinner. The holiday season was a dreadful time of year to be without a penny. Try as she would to conceal her disappointment her lip trembled.

When Hal met her that night and they started home she could hardly utter a syllable. It was not alone her own trouble that depressed her. She longed and yet dreaded to hear what had befallen her brother. Were a calamity like hers to come to him then indeed had misfortune descended upon the Harling household. How would the invalid mother and the feeble old grandfather get on without money? How would medicines be procured? Or the rent be paid?

Hal, however, was to all appearances his serene self. He talked and jested quite in his usual manner and if he were keeping something back he certainly succeeded in doing so to perfection. Perhaps, argued she, he had not been discharged at all. If not, why should this disgrace have come to her? For in a measure it was a disgrace. When you lost your job in the mill all Baileyville knew it and discussed the circumstances, weighing the justice or injustice of the act. Certainly, thought Louise to herself, she had toiled as faithfully as she knew how. Had there been fault with her work at least she was not conscious of it. It was mortifying, galling, to be turned away without a word of explanation.

"What's the matter, Sis?" Hal questioned, at last noticing that his chatter failed to elicit its usual a gay response.

Louise hesitated, shrinking from putting her tidings into words.

"You look as if you'd seen a ghost, old girl," smiled her brother facetiously. "What's up?"

"I've been—they don't want——"

Hal halted, aghast.

"You don't mean to say they've asked you to quit?"

"Yes."

The boy's eyes blazed.

"It's Corcoran, the cur! He's done it to get back at me for what I said to him."

"You think so?"

"Sure!"

"But why choose me? I had nothing to do with the squabble."

"That's just the point. He's smart enough to know it would hit me a darn sight harder to have you lose your job than to lose my own," blustered her brother wrathfully.

"I wish I was sure it was only that."

"Why?"

"Because then I wouldn't care so much. I should know there was nothing the matter with my work."

"Of course there isn't. You're one of the best operators they've got in the mill. Hines, one of the bosses, told me so only the other day."

"Really?" The girl's face brightened. "Why didn't you tell me?"

"Oh, I don't know. Forgot it, I guess," smiled Hal. It was not his way to pass on compliments. Had the criticism been adverse he would have told it quickly enough.

"Well, I'm awfully glad he said so."

"Yes, it was very decent of him. Everybody knows though that you're a fine worker—even old Corcoran himself, I'll be bound, although he wouldn't admit it. You're quick, careful, prompt and never absent. What else do they want? Oh, Corcoran was behind this, all right. It wasn't your work sacked you. It was plain spite."

"I'm thankful for that!" sighed Louise.

"I'm not. It makes me hot," burst out Hal.

"Still, it is better than losing your place because your work was so poor you couldn't hold the job," smiled the girl.

"I can't see it that way. This is just low down and unfair."

"But I don't mind that. I know I wasn't to blame."

"You bet you weren't. I wish I had Corcoran here. I'd shake the daylights out of him."

"Whose daylights are going to be shaken out now?" inquired a laughing voice, and the brother and sister turned to see Carl McGregor beside them.

"Old Corcoran up at the works," snarled Hal. "He's given Louise the sack!"

Carl did not speak. He knew only too well how genuine was this disaster. In the sympathetic silence that followed the three young persons seemed to draw closer together.

"It isn't as if Loulie had done anything to deserve such a slam," Hal suddenly declared. "He's just taking out his spite on me and he's chosen this means of doing it. To light on a woman! I'd a hundred times rather he'd shipped me. But it's like him."

Moodily the three walked on.

"Of course, I must get some other place right away," Louise said presently, as if thinking aloud. "I don't know just what. I've never worked anywhere but in the mills and I have no other trade. To be turned away from Davis and Coulter won't be much of a recommendation for me either, I'm afraid."

"Oh, you can get a hundred jobs," announced Hal, with a confidence he did not feel. "Don't you fret."

"I don't know." His sister shook her head. "Scores of Baileyville girls are idle."

The statement met with no denial. Who could combat it? It was only too true.

"Not girls like you," Carl ventured, determined to be optimistic.

"Girls exactly like me, Carlie," smiled Louise.

"Oh, you won't be idle," murmured Hal.

"I can't be—I simply can't. We've got to have money."

Once again her companions found themselves unable to refute the declaration.

They had turned into the main thoroughfare of the town and were threading their way along a sidewalk teeming with the throng of Saturday shoppers that is such a characteristic part of the life of a mill town. The street beside them was black with trucks, motor cars, and the congested traffic of a manufacturing center.

Suddenly there was a cry from Carl.

"Jove!" exclaimed he. "Look at that kid!"

In his horror he put out his hand to clutch his friend's arm. But his fingers closed on empty air.

Hal Harling was gone!

What followed happened so quickly that it was more like the shiftings of a moving picture than an incident in real life.

Hal bounded into the seething maelstrom of the street, caught up a little boy midway in the stream of rushing vehicles and held him aloft in safety.

The baby had obviously been pursuing a small black puppy whose dangling leash told a story of escape from captivity. Making the most of his freedom the dog had run recklessly along and the child had dashed after him, too intent on recapturing his pet to heed whither the chase took him. It was little short of a miracle that he had not been killed and for his rescue from such a fate he had the quick wit of Hal Harling to thank.

A second later all passing on the street had stopped and crowds of spectators surged around the young hero. Above the tense stillness could be heard Hal's comforting voice:

"Sure we'll find your dog for you, little chap. Don't cry. You say he's called Midget. That's a fine name for a dog, isn't it? See! Somebody over there on the sidewalk has him already. We'll go and get him."

As the two chubby arms closed about Hal's neck into the center of the crowd catapulted a frenzied nursemaid who madly rushed up to young Harling.

"He's not hurt a mite," Hal announced, reassuringly. "I guess he ran away from you, didn't he?"

"He was leading the dog and the leash slipped out of his hands," gasped the affrighted girl. "Before I'd a notion what he was going to do he was off after the puppy. I'm weak as a rag. If anything had happened to him——"

"But it didn't," smiled Hal.

"No, thanks to you, and to the good Lord!"

Then, seizing the child in her arms, she said:

"There, Billie, you see what comes of running out of the yard after Midget. You might have been killed but for this kind gentleman."

"Indeed he might! He would have been. I saw the whole thing myself," broke in a policeman who had joined the group.

"I'm glad he's all right," reiterated Hal, as he gave the child into the maid's care.

A man approached leading Midget and interest being for the moment diverted from himself Hal made his escape.

In a doorway he spied Louise and Carl.

"Oh, it was wonderful of you, Hal!" his sister murmured.

"It was just lucky," Hal returned a bit gruffly. "Come on! Let's get out of this push. We'll be late for supper if we don't hike along."

And it was characteristic of Hal Harling that this was the only allusion he made to the adventure.

CHAPTER IV

PROBLEMS

Although temporarily buoyed up by the episode of the afternoon Carl McGregor returned home with spirits at a lower ebb than they had been for many a day. To be out of work was a very real tragedy in the world in which he lived. He knew only too well how indispensable was money and that the necessity of it was even greater in the Harling home than in his own. The Harlings, alas, had no absent Uncle Frederick to fall back upon. On the contrary the entire upkeep of their home and family fell upon the young shoulders of the boy and girl who toiled at the spinning mills. Now with Louise out of the race Hal would be left alone with all the burden, and whether he would be able to carry so heavy a one was a question. Undoubtedly he would not be forced to bear it for long. Louise would find employment—she must find it. Did not the need compel it? And was she not far too capable a worker to be out of a place? Why, scores of people would seek her help eagerly when once it was known her assistance was available.

Sound as these arguments were, however, facts did not bear them out. Apparently nobody in Baileyville wished help, no matter how excellent its quality. Every night the report from the Harlings was the same—Louise could find nothing to do. Even Mrs. McGregor who was ordinarily able to straighten out every sort of tangle had no remedy for the present pitiable dilemma. The only employment it was in her power to secure for the girl was fine sewing and Louise, restricted by her factory training, could not sew. A week went by and still nothing presented itself. Mrs. Harling and the aged grandfather, from whom the calamity had been kept as long as it was possible to conceal it, at length took up the worry.

"Whatever is going to become of us now?" bewailed each in turn. "Where's the food and rent coming from?"

Hal fidgeted.

Every day he looked more harrowed and distressed, and the smile that had formerly come so spontaneously came now with an effort. He had taken on an extra job evenings, that of delivery boy for the local grocer. It did not bring in much, to be sure, and it kept him on his feet at the end of the day when often he was too tired to stand. However, all these disadvantages were lost sight of in the few additional dollars derived from the makeshift.

"Mother says you can't keep this up, old chap," remarked Carl dismally. "She says you will be getting tired out and sick and then where will you be?"

"But we've got to have the cash, kid! *Got to have it*, don't you see? It was I who landed us in this plight and I'm the one to get us out. It's nobody's fault but mine."

Carl sighed.

"I suppose Corcoran wouldn't——"

"Take Louise back if I were to humble myself," flared Hal. "Do you think for a moment I'd ask him? Do you imagine I'd gratify him by letting him know how hard he'd hit us? Not on your life! For all he knows the Harlings are rich as mud and don't care a hurrah for his old job. I want him to think that too. If he pictures me eating out of his hand he's mistaken."

Carl looked grave.

"It is all very well to be proud," affirmed he, smiling at his friend's characteristic attitude of mind. "But sometimes you can't afford to be too cocky. If, as you say, you pitched into Corcoran and were wrong——"

"But I wasn't wrong," broke in Hal. "I meant every word I said; it was the truth and I'd say it again if I got the chance. You'd have said the same yourself if you'd been there. The thing that got his goat was that it was true."

"But you can't go round telling people the truth about themselves, old man," observed Carl with a wisdom far beyond his years. "They won't stand for it."

"I'll bet I would. I'd a darn sight rather a person told me straight to my face what he thought of me than whispered it behind my back."

"That's what I'm trying to do now," grinned Carl.

Young Harling's lips curved into a smile.

"Why, so you are, kid," returned he. "I didn't recognize the stunt at first. You're a mighty white little chap, Carl. Maybe I was wrong to light into Corcoran as I did. Of course he is my superior and I really had no business to sarse him, even if he was wrong. But he is such a cad! It made my blood boil to hear him berate that poor little Mayo girl—and for something she did not do, too."

"I know."

"Well, if you were in this mess what would you do? Come now. Give me some of your sage advice."

"You don't suppose you ought to go to——"

"Corcoran and apologize?" interrupted Hal hotly. "No, I don't. I'd starve before I'd do that."

"But how about your grandfather, your mother, and Louise?"

"I shan't let them starve, if that's what you mean. You can bet your life on that," cried Hal. "If anybody goes without it will be myself."

"You seem to be doing it all right."

"How do you know?"

"Don't you suppose I've eyes in my head? You're thin as a rail already."

"Huh! That's only because I've been chasing round with bundles. I was too fat, anyway; didn't get enough exercise at the mills."

"Hal Harling!"

"Straight goods, I didn't. Just stood and fed stuff into that loom from morning till night. You don't call that exercise, do you?"

"I noticed that by night you were often all in, exercise or no exercise," was the dry response. "Well, you've got to go your own gait, I guess."

"I'll bet a hat *you* wouldn't go and bow down to Corcoran."

The thrust told.

"Bow down to him? I'd crack his nut!"

Hal chuckled with satisfaction at his chum's loyalty.

"There you are, you see!" declared he. "You are every whit as rabid as I am when it comes to the scratch."

"I'm afraid I'm more rabid when things hit you and Louise," murmured Carl.

The two walked on without speaking, the mind of each busy with the problem in hand.

Carl's imagination circled every mad avenue of escape from the Harlings' financial crisis. If only he were rich! If only somebody would suddenly leave him some money! If only—his brain halted in the midst of its absurd gyrations.

If he were not rich; if he had no fairy fortune to pass over to Hal and Louise, what was to hinder him from performing for them a far more genuine service of friendship and affection? Instead of offering them money that was dropped into his hand why should he not test out his real regard for them by earning it? Many a boy his age, aye, younger than he, earned money. Why should he be free of responsibility when Hal, who was only a few years older, was weighed down with it?

Just why it had never occurred to him that if he earned money he might with propriety hand it over to his own hard-working mother is a question. Often with eyes fixed on the clouds we lose sight of the things just beneath our noses. Perhaps that was the explanation of Carl's lack of thought. Be that as it may, certain it was that he parted from his chum afire with the generous impulse of making a personal effort to reinforce the Harlings' slender income.

He was only a stone's throw from home and what led him to turn the other way, pass into Beaver Street, and go south toward Orient Avenue he could not have told. Possibly he was still thrilling with newly awakened altruism and was not yet ready to have his roseate dreams disturbed. Or he may have been pondering so deeply how to put his impulses into action that he failed to heed just where he was going. At any rate before he realized it there he was in the fashionable section of the village, walking along between rows of bare and stately elms and great rambling houses glimpsed from behind high brick walls.

He had not been in this part of Baileyville for months. There was nothing to take him there. What connection had his life with those fortunate lives that made leisure and luxury things to be taken for granted? Even now he started at finding himself in a location so incongruous; or rather at finding so incongruous a person as himself in an environment so out of harmony with his thought and station.

He whirled about to start homeward and it was just at this instant that a trim racing car drew up beside him and a man's voice inquired pleasantly:

"Lost your way, youngster?"

Carl glanced at the speaker.

He was a gray-haired, clean-shaven man, with fresh color and keen blue eyes. Although muffled to the chin in a raccoon coat that almost met the fur of his cap there was a splendid vigor about him that breathed health, energy, and the rewards a temperate life brings. Everything about him seemed clearness personified—eye, complexion, voice.

"I've not lost my way, thank you, sir," Carl answered. "I just got to thinking and have wandered farther from home than I meant to."

"Are you going back to town now?"

"Yes, sir."

"Jump in and I'll give you a lift."

Raising the fur robes invitingly the stranger reached to open the door.

Carl was almost too surprised to speak.

"You're very kind, sir," he contrived to stammer. "I should be glad of a ride. I don't often get one. Besides, I ought to have been at home long ago."

The honesty of the reply apparently pleased the motorist for, smiling, he tucked the lad in and asked:

"Where do you live?"

"At Mulberry Court, sir."

"I'm afraid I don't quite know where that is."

"Very likely not. It's a little tenement house off Minton Street. Maybe you never were there."

"I guess I never was," the man replied simply.

"It's a nice place to live," continued Carl, glowing with local pride. "Of course it isn't like this. We've no trees. But in winter trees aren't much good anyway; and in summer we can go to the parks."

To this philosophic observation his companion agreed with a nod and they sped on in silence.

The vast stretches of snow, so unsightly in the city's narrow thoroughfares, were on every hand white and sparkling, and each little shrub rearing its head out of the spangled fields was laden with ermine.

The boy drew a long breath, drinking in the crystal air.

"Gee!" he burst out impulsively. "This is great. I feel cheered up already."

The man driving the car shot him a quiet smile.

"I'm glad to hear that," said he. "So you were out of spirits, were you?"

"I was fussed within an inch of my life," owned Carl with engaging candor.

"In wrong somewhere?"

"Oh, I'm not; but my chum is."

"What's the matter?"

"Why, you see his sister has just been fired from Davis and Coulter's mills. It wasn't her fault at all, either. Her brother gave the foreman, Corcoran, a jawing because he got too fresh with one of the girls. Corcoran didn't say a word at the time but a couple of weeks later he took out his spite on Hal Harling's sister, Louise. I suppose he was mad and decided on this way to get even."

"Humph!"

"Maybe he thought he'd take Hal's pride down and make him come crawling to him on his knees to get Louise back into the mills. It is a rotten time to be out of work. Louise has tried and tried to get another job and can't land a thing. But whether she does or not, her brother isn't going crawling to Corcoran. He's not afraid of the old tyrant. Hal Harling isn't afraid of anything. Why, only the other day he tore into the street and saved a little runaway chap from being mashed to jelly under a lot of automobiles. The baby was chasing a dog and got into the middle of High Street before he realized it. He would certainly have been killed had it not been for Hal."

"Whose baby was it?" questioned the man beside him in an odd voice.

"Oh, I don't know. We didn't wait to see. Hal was anxious to get out of the crowd and we were late home anyway. So Harling gave the kid to the nursemaid and lit out."

There was a muffled: "I see!" from his listener.

"And where do you come in in all this tangle?" queried the stranger presently.

"I? Why, you see Hal Harling is my——" a sudden reserve fell upon the lad. It was impossible to explain to anybody just what Hal Harling was to him. "I chase round with the Harlings a lot," explained he. "They are almost like my own family."

"Oh, so that's it!"

"I'd decided just now to hunt for a job and see if I couldn't make good the money Louise is missing. She can't seem to find a darn thing to do, poor kid. She's been out of work over a week now and they've got to have money or Mrs. Harling and Grandfather Harling will starve to death. Of course I'm not so much," continued Carl modestly. "But I'm willing to work and I'm sure I could earn something."

The owner of the velvet-wheeled car did not speak at once. Then he remarked abruptly:

"You don't go to school to-morrow, do you?"

"Saturday? Not on your—no, sir."

"Then you'd be free to come to my office to-morrow morning and see me, wouldn't you?"

"Do you think you could give me a job? Sure I'd come!" ejaculated Carl with zest.

"Good! Come to the Berwick building, Number 197 Dalby Street, to-morrow at ten o'clock. Give your name and—by the by, what is your name?"

"Carl McGregor, sir."

"A fine old Scotch name. Well, you write it on a card or a piece of paper and give it to the man you will find at the door. Maybe I shall be able to do something for you."

The car rolled up to the curb and stopped.

"You've been mighty kind, sir," said Carl, as he leaped out. "You've brought me nearly home."

"Oh, I was going this way anyway," smiled the man in the fur coat. "You won't have far to walk now, will you?"

"Only a block. I'll be home in a jiffy."

"You won't forget about to-morrow."

"*Forget!*"

Laughing at something that evidently amused him very much the stranger started his engine.

As for Carl, he raced home as fast as ever his feet would go. Already he was late for supper, a fact always annoying to his mother, who considered tardiness one of the most flagrant of sins. To be sure he was not often late, for miss what other functions he might he seldom missed his meals. To-night, however, the table had been cleared, the dishes washed, and only a saucepan of corn-meal mush, steaming on the back of the stove, remained as a souvenir of the feast.

"For goodness' sake, Carl, wherever have you been?" asked Mrs. McGregor, as he entered, panting from his run up the long flights of stairs. "I've been worried to death about you. Go wash your hands and come and eat your supper right away. You know I don't like you out after dark."

"I know it, Ma," the boy responded penitently. "I'm mighty sorry. I'd no idea, though, that it was so late."

"Where've you been?"

"To walk."

"To walk? Just to walk? Mercy on us! Not just walking round for nothing!"

"I'm afraid so, yes."

"Who was with you?"

"Nobody."

For an instant Mrs. McGregor looked searchingly at her son.

"Well, did you ever hear the like of that!" commented she, addressing the younger children who clustered about their brother with curiosity. "What set you to go walking?"

"I don't know, Ma. Just a freak, I guess."

"A foolish freak—worrying the whole family, delaying supper, and what not. Now come and eat your porridge without more delay. Mary, go bring the milk; and, Timmie, you fetch a clean saucer from the pantry. Martin, stop pestering your brother until he eats something; he'll play with you and Nell by and by. Such a noisy lot of bairns as you are! If you're not careful you'll wake James Frederick."

Nevertheless, in spite of her grumbling, the mother regarded her brood of clamoring youngsters with affectionate pride. They were indeed a husky group, red-cheeked, high-spirited, and happy; their chatter, as she well knew, was nothing more than the normal exuberance of childhood.

While Carl hungrily devoured his big bowlful of cereal his mother continued her sewing. She was working on a film of blue material a-glitter with silver beads that twinkled from its folds like stars. Every now and then little Nell, fascinated by the sparkle of the fabric, would start toward the corner where her mother sat in the ring of brilliant lamplight.

Instantly one of the older brothers or sisters would intercept the child, catching up the wriggling mite and explaining softly:

"No, dearie, no! Nell must not trouble mother. Mother's working."

It was an old, oft-repeated formula which every one of the little group had heard from the time he had been able to toddle. Familiar, too, was the picture of their mother seated in the circle of light, her basket of gayly hued spools beside her, and a cloud of shimmering splendor wreathing her feet. Sometimes this glory was pink; sometimes it was blue, lavender, or yellow; not infrequently it was black or a smoky mist of gray. The children always delighted in the brighter colors, crowding round with eagerness whenever a new gown was brought home to see what hue the exciting parcel might contain.

"Oh, nothing but a sleepy old gray one this time!" Timmie would bewail. "And gray beads, too! Do hurry up, Ma, and get it done so we can have something else."

But let the paper disclose a brilliant blue or a red tulle and instantly every child clapped his hands.

Exultantly they examined the scintillating jet or iridescent sequins.

"Oh, this is the best yet, Ma!" Carl would cry. "It's a peach of a dress."

Their ingenious admiration did much to transform their mother's tedious task into a fine art and helped her to regard it with dignity. Certainly its influence on the characters of her children was inestimable. Not alone did it answer their craving for beauty, but far better than this æsthetic gratification was the education it gave them in thoughtfulness and unselfishness. Consideration for their mother, restraint, independence, all emerged out of the yards of foolish gauze and the frivolous spangles.

Therefore Mrs. McGregor sewed on serene in spirit and if, as to-night, her task barred her from secrets her children might amid greater leisure have bestowed on her, the circumstance was accepted as one of the unavoidable disadvantages attending constant occupation.

It was regrettable she had not more time to talk with her sons and daughters separately. Confidences were shy and volatile things that could not be delivered in a hurry or hastily fitted into the chinks of a busy day. Confidences depended on mood and could not be regulated so that they would be forthcoming in the few seconds snatched between one duty and another.

As a result it came about that after Carl had swallowed his supper, frolicked with the younger children and helped Mary put them to bed, brought in the kindlings and coal for the morning fire, it was time for him to tumble in between the sheets himself, and he did so without mentioning to his mother or any one else his adventures of the afternoon or his morrow's appointment with the stranger.

One does not always wish to relate his affairs before five

small brothers and sisters whose little ears drink in the story and whose tiny tongues are liable artlessly to repeat it.

In the McGregor household there was affection and happiness; but, alas, there was no such thing as privacy.

CHAPTER V

A TANGLE OF SURPRISES

Morning, to which Carl had looked forward for a moment with his mother, brought, alas, even more meager opportunity for imparting secrets than had the night before, for as was the custom of the McGregor family the new day was launched amid a turmoil of confusion. Hence it came about that although Carl made several valiant attempts to waylay his mother in the pantry, or corral her in her room, he was each time thwarted and was never able to get beyond a vague introduction to the topic so near his heart. At length a multitudinous list of errands to the butcher, grocer, and baker was handed him and there was no alternative but catch up his hat and coat and speed forth upon these commissions. And no sooner were they all fulfilled than the hour for his appointment with the stranger arrived and, palpitating with the interest of his mission, he set forth to the address to which he had been directed.

It was in the down-town part of the village and so busy was he dodging trucks and hurrying pedestrians that he paid scant heed to anything but the gilt numbers that dotted the street. In and out the crowd he wove his way until above a doorway the magic characters he sought stared at him.

There may have been, and probably were, signs announcing

the nature of the business in which this mysterious friend was engaged but if so Carl was blind to them. All that concerned him was to find the place that sheltered his remarkable acquaintance and ascertain the sequel of the day before.

Therefore he walked timidly into the hallway and seeing at the other end of it an oaken door panelled with ground glass that bore the hieroglyphics of his quest he turned the heavy brass knob and walked in.

The room was spacious and its rich furnishings and atmosphere of stillness were in such marked contrast to the hubbub of the street that he paused on the heavy rug, abashed. There was, however, no time for retreat even had his courage failed him for the door behind him had no sooner clicked together than a boy in a gray uniform came forward. As he approached his eye swept with disapproval the shabby visitor and he said, with an edge of sharpness crisping his tone:

"What can I do for you?"

"I want to see a—a—gentleman," stammered Carl. "I don't know his name. I forgot to ask it. But he told me to come to this number to-day at ten o'clock and give him my name on a piece of paper. I've got it here somewheres."

Awkwardly he searched his pockets, the waiting messenger watching his every movement.

It was a grimy morsel of parchment that was at length produced; but the instant the supercilious page read the name scrawled upon it his attitude changed from superiority to servility.

"This way, sir, if you please," said he, wheeling about.

Carl followed his guide, feeling, as he tagged across the silencing rug, deplorably small, and painfully conscious of both his hands and feet. He and his conductor passed through another door, threaded labyrinthian aisles flanked by gaping clerks and faintly smiling stenographers, and came at length to a third door which the youth preceding him opened with a flourish.

"Mr. Carl McGregor," announced he in a stentorian tone.

All the blood in Carl's body rushed to his face.

The room before him was small and on its warmly tinted walls a few pictures, some of which his school training led him to recognize as Rembrandt reproductions, lent charm and interest to the interior. But these details were of minor importance compared to the thrill he experienced at discovering behind a great mahogany desk the mysterious stranger of his motoring adventure.

Yes, it was he—there could be no question about that. And yet, now that his hat and heavy fur coat were removed he appeared surprisingly slender and youthful. His eyes, too, seemed bluer, his cheeks redder, and his mouth more smiling.

"Well, shaver, you're prompt," announced he, pointing to the clock with evident satisfaction.

"You said ten, sir."

"So I did. Nevertheless, I often say ten and get quarter past ten or even eleven o'clock. Sit down."

He motioned toward a huge leather chair at his elbow and slipping into it the boy perched with anticipation on its forward edge.

"Well, what about that Miss Harling we were talking of yesterday? Has she a position yet?"

"Since last night, you mean? I don't know, sir. I haven't seen any of the Harlings to-day. But I hardly think so."

The stranger pursed his lips.

"Too bad! Too bad!" he murmured. "And you are still for helping the family out by taking a job, are you?"

"If I can get one; yes, sir."

"Just what kind of work had you in mind?"

"Why—I—I—hadn't thought about it."

"I suppose you go to school."

"Yes, sir. That's the dickens of it. My mother makes me. I'd a great deal rather go into Davis and Coulter's cotton mills. Lots of boys and girls my age do go there, and that is where my father worked before he died. But Ma is hot on education. She says I've got to have one, and she insists on sewing at home on all sorts of fool flummeries for some dressmaker so I can. It's rotten of me not to be more pleased about it, I suppose."

While Carl fumbled with his cap the man at the desk tilted back in his chair, regarding him narrowly.

"Your school work can't leave you very much time for anything else," remarked he.

"Oh, yes, it does," the lad hastened to retort. "I have Saturdays and—and—spare hours at night. I'd even work Sundays if there was anything I could do."

"At that rate I am afraid you would not find much time for skating or baseball. People have to have fresh air and exercise, you know, to keep well."

"I don't have to play," protested Carl with great earnestness. "Anyhow I get heaps of exercise and fresh air doing errands. Besides, we live up five flights."

His listener turned aside his head.

"If it comes to exercise I get all I want right at home," persisted the boy. "I've a crew of little brothers and sisters, too, and when I'm not busy I help take care of them so Ma can sew. Just you try doing it once if you are looking for exercise. And then I wheel the baby out."

There was a twinkle in the eye of the man at the desk but he said gravely:

"Isn't it going to bother them at home if you take a position? How does your mother feel about it?"

"I haven't had a chance to ask her," Carl blurted out with honesty. "All last evening she was rushing to finish that spangled thing; and this morning she had the kids to dress and I had errands to do. It's awful hard to get a chance to talk to Ma by herself. Some of the children are always clawing at her skirts and bothering her."

"You do believe, though, in talking things over with your mother."

"Sure! We always tell Ma everything if we can get a chance. So does all Mulberry Court, for that matter. Ma's that sort."

The stranger toyed with an ivory letter-opener thoughtfully.

"Now I'll tell you what we'll do," began he at last. "To-day is Saturday, isn't it?"

Carl nodded.

"Well, if your friends, the Harlings, are not straightened out by Monday morning I will let you begin a week from to-day as errand boy in this office."

"Bully!" cried the delighted applicant.

"If, on the other hand," continued the gentleman at the desk, speaking slowly and evenly, and not heeding the interruption, "Miss Harling finds work and the family do not need your aid, you must agree to put in your free time at home helping your mother as you have been doing in the past. Is that a bargain?"

"Y-e-s."

"What's the matter?"

"It just seems to me we might as well settle it definitely now that I am to come here next week. To-day is Saturday and I don't believe Louise will find work before Monday morning. Of course she can't do anything about getting a job Sunday."

Although there was a perceptible tremor of disappointment in the boy's voice the stranger appeared not to notice it. Rising, he put out his hand with a kindly smile.

"I am afraid the agreement I have made with you is the best I can do at present," said he. "I will be true to my part of it if you will be true to yours. I promise you that if the Harlings' affairs do not take an upward turn by Monday you shall come to their rescue."

"Thank you, sir."

"I wouldn't worry any more about this, if I were you, sonny," concluded the man. "Go home and try to be satisfied. I'll keep the place for you, remember. It is Carl McGregor, isn't it, of——"

"Mulberry Court—the top flat."

"And did you tell me these friends of yours, the Harlings, lived there too?"

"Oh, no, sir! I wish they did. The Harlings are at Number 40 Broad Street. It is the corner house. They took the tenement because there was sun, and because it entertains Grandfather and Mrs. Harling to look out the window. They can't ever go out and it cheers them up to have something to see. It costs more to live there than where we do, but Hal and Louise decided it was worth it."

"Under the circumstances I imagine it is," assented the stranger. "Well, we will wish them luck."

"I hope they have it!"

"So do I." As he spoke the man pressed a bell in answer to which the uniformed page appeared.

"Show this young gentleman out, Billie," said he. "Good-by, youngster! Good-by!"

The farewell was cordial and in its cadence rang so disconcerting a finality that try as he might Carl could not repress a conviction that in spite of his suave promises his new-found friend did not really expect to see him again.

"I guess there are folks like that," meditated he, as he walked dispiritedly home. "They are awful pleasant to your face and give you the feeling they are going to do wonders for you. But when it comes to the scratch they slide from under. This chap is one of that slick bunch, I'll bet a hat."

It was not a cheering reflection and with every step lower and lower ebbed his hopes. It chanced that his pathway to Mulberry Court led past the corner of Broad Street (or if it did not really lead him there his subconscious mind did) and once in the vicinity what more natural than that he should drop in at Number 40 to pass the time of day? Grandfather Harling loved to have visitors. He said they cheered him up.

But to-day neither the old gentleman nor any of the Harling family needed cheering. Carl found them in such high spirits that for a time it was difficult to get any of the group to talk coherently.

"What do you suppose has happened, Carl?" cried Louise, the instant he was inside the door. "The most wonderful thing! You never could guess if you guessed forever."

"If it is as hopeless as that I shan't try," laughed Carl.

"But it is amazing, a miracle!" put in Mrs. Harling.

"We can't understand it at all," quavered Grandfather Harling, who was quite as excited as the rest.

"Well, what *is* it?" the boy demanded.

"You'll never believe it," laughed Louise with shining eyes. "I've had a letter. You couldn't guess who it's from!"

She held a square white envelope high above her head.

"I'm going to have it framed and hand it down to my great-great-grandchildren."

"You might let me see it," coaxed Carl, putting out his hand.

"Oh, it is far too precious to be touched. It is going to be an archive, an heirloom, you know."

"Oh, come on and tell a chap what's happened," urged Carl, his patience beginning to wane.

"Well, think of this! I've had a note from Mr. Coulter—not from the firm, understand, but from the great J. W. himself, written by his own hand. He says he hears that through some error my name has been dropped from the Davis and Coulter payroll, and he not only asks me to come back to the mill but sends me a cheek for double the sum that I have lost by being out. Can you beat that?"

"Oh, Louise, how bully! I *am* glad! But how do you suppose——"

"That's exactly what we don't know. It seems like magic, doesn't it? I never knew before that Mr. Coulter kept such close track of what went on at the mills. He doesn't come there often because he is always at the down-town office. When he does visit the mills he simply strolls through them as if they belonged to somebody else rather than to himself. Of course he doesn't know one of the workers and I've always fancied he didn't care much about us. But this proves how wrong I was to think so. He does care, you see, and means everybody shall have a square deal. I shall go back Monday and work harder than ever for him. You will work your fingers off for such a man as that, you know."

"It certainly is white of him!" Carl agreed.

"It is nothing but justice," asserted Mrs. Harling proudly. "Still, justice isn't a common commodity in this world."

"Evidently it isn't Mr. Coulter's fault if it isn't, Mother," Louise replied. "And isn't it nice, Carl, that I am not to go back to work under Mr. Corcoran. Oh, I forgot to tell you that. That is almost the best of all. No! I am to be in the shipping department where the work is lighter and the pay better. Won't Hal be tickled to death when he hears it? He'll be more convinced than ever that he did the right thing to lay Corcoran out."

"I think he did. Still, it was a dangerous experiment and this should be a warning to him," put in Mrs. Harling. "Hal must learn to be more careful with his temper, his tongue, and those fists of his. If he isn't he is going to get into serious trouble some day."

Carl, however, was not listening to Mrs. Harling's moralizing.

"I wish I knew how Mr. Coulter found out about Louise," murmured he, half aloud.

Well, this was certainly a most satisfactory termination to the Harlings' troubles. He was genuinely glad the affair had turned so fortunately. And yet in his heart lurked a vague regret. This would mean that probably he would never see or hear from the mysterious hero of the red racing car again. Could the stranger have had any knowledge of what was to happen and did that information account for his jaunty adieu? Of course such a thing was impossible. And yet how odd and puzzling it all was!

CHAPTER VI

THE WEB WIDENS

W herever did you disappear to?" inquired his mother when, hungry but triumphant, Carl came home. "I've been looking everywhere for you."

"I didn't know you wanted me this morning, Ma," the boy replied, an afterglow of happiness still on his face.

"I didn't really want you but I wanted to know where you were. I've asked you time and time again when you go out to tell me where you're going."

"I wanted to, Mother, but it was such a long story. Last night you were too busy to hear it; and this morning there was no chance to talk to you either."

He heard his mother sigh.

"It's a pretty kind of a life I lead if my own children can't get a minute to talk to me."

"But you are busy, Ma. You know you are."

"I certainly do. Nobody knows it better," replied the woman with a sad shake of her head.

Carl, sensing the regret in her tone, hastened to say:

"Well, at least the family is not so thick around here now as usual. Where is everybody?"

"Mary is out with James Frederick; Timmie has gone

to the park to coast; and Martin and Nell are at the day nursery."

"Then we have it all to ourselves."

"For a second or two, yes."

"That's bully!"

Drawing up a kitchen chair he sat down beside his mother.

"It's nice to have them gone sometimes," remarked he. "The kids make such a racket."

"They'll not always be making it," returned Mrs. McGregor philosophically. "And anyway, the three of them put together can never equal the hullabaloo you used to make when you were their age."

"I'm quiet enough now," grinned Carl sheepishly.

"Quiet, you call it, do you? Quiet! And you prancing home from every ball game with a black eye or else the clothes half torn off you!" She chuckled mischievously. "But you're not telling me where you've been. Up to some deviltry, I'll be bound, or you wouldn't be so anxious to get it off your conscience."

"I haven't been up to any high jinks this time, Ma," protested the lad soberly. "You'll see when I tell you."

Slowly he related his story while his mother bent over her needle, spangling with brilliants a gauze of azure hue. She was a wonderful listener, sympathetic in her intentness.

When the boy had finished her hand wandered to touch his rough sleeve.

"A kind deed is never amiss in the world," observed she briefly. "If we would but pass on to other folks the kindness people do to us the world would soon become a pleasanter place. I'm thankful to know Louise has her job back, or rather that she has a better one. She's a good girl and deserves it. Besides, with Christmas coming, it would be hard to be without money."

"And Mr. Coulter—wasn't he great? And wasn't it all funny?"

"Funny is hardly the word; but I'll agree that Mr. Coulter was great. It is always great for a big man to take on his soul the troubles of those needier than himself. Well, he's done a good deed this day and may he be the happier for it. And he will be—never fear! I wonder how he got wind of the trouble Louise was in? You don't suppose———" She halted a moment as if suddenly struck by a new thought; then she laughed and shrugged her shoulders, "Of course it couldn't be—how ridiculous! Well, anyway, it is splendid everything has come out so well. And now that you're here, sonny, would you mind fetching some coal from the shed and starting up the fire for dinner? Mary'll be back soon and 'twould be a nice surprise for her to find the kettle boiling."

"So it would!" answered Carl, leaping up to do his mother's bidding.

"I'm not forgetting you'd like to do a bit of coasting or skating to-day," Mrs. McGregor continued. "If you will fit in a few errands early in the afternoon I'll let you off at two o'clock for a holiday."

"That will be great, Ma! But—but don't you———"

"It will be all right, sonny. Tim has had his play this morning and he shall help the rest of the day. Hush a minute! Isn't that Mrs. O'Dowd's knock? Very like she's up to ask me to run down and see little Katie who is laid up with a sore throat. Well, I'll go but I won't be long. Meantime if you can lend Mary a hand dinner will be through the quicker and you will be off to play the earlier."

Thus it happened that before two o'clock Carl McGregor was one of the shouting throng of boys that crowded the small pond in Davis Park. Amid swirling skaters and a confusion of hockey sticks he moved in and out of the thick of the game. So intent was he upon the sport that he might have continued playing until dark had not a boy at his elbow suddenly piped:

"There goes Hal Harling! Hi, Hal! Come on down!"

"Harling! Harling!" cried the other boys, taking up the call.

"Come on and play, Hal! You can have Sanderson's skates. He's going home."

"Can't do it!" laughed the giant, waving his hand.

"Oh, come on, old top!"

"Not to-night, fellers! Got to go home."

"I've got to see Harling!" Carl exclaimed, hurriedly loosening his skates.

"You're not going, too!"

"Got to. So long! Hold on, Hal! I'm coming with you."

Scrambling up the bank, Carl overtook his friend.

"Hullo, Carlie! What struck you to quit?" asked he unceremoniously.

"Time I was getting home. Besides, I wanted to see you."

A smile passed between them.

"To tell the truth, I hoped I'd spy you somewhere, kid. I've got great news! Corcoran has been fired! What do you know about that?"

"Corcoran!"

"The old man himself—no other!"

"Jove! Why, I thought you said he'd been at the mills all his life."

"So he has."

"But—but—to fire him now!"

"Well, he hasn't actually been fired," amended young Harling, "but so far as I'm concerned it amounts to the same thing. He's been transferred to another department and he isn't to be a boss any more, poor old chap!"

"But aren't you glad?" questioned Carl with surprise.

"Why, yes, in some ways," returned Hal thoughtfully. "Yes, of course I'm glad not to have him sarsing the girls and pestering me. Still, I'm sort of sorry for him."

"*Sorry?*"

Hal nodded.

"But I thought you——"

"I know! I know! I'm not saying he wasn't an awful old screw. But somehow I don't believe he meant to be so flinty-hearted. You see, he came and talked to me to-day—talked like a regular human being. You could have knocked me over. It seems—a funny thing—that kid I picked up out of the street the other day was his."

"Corcoran's kid!"

"Yep! Can you beat it? Of course I hadn't a notion who the little tike belonged to; but even if I had I should have done the same thing. You wouldn't let a kid like that be run over no matter who his father was."

"But—but—Corcoran!" gasped Carl. "How did he know it was you who rescued his baby?"

"Somebody told him. He said it cut him up terribly because of the way he'd treated Louise."

"Served him right."

"Maybe! But he was cut up, poor old cuss! You'd have been sorry for him yourself, if you'd heard him. He isn't all brute by any means. Why, when he spoke about his little boy——"

"But Louise!"

"I know. It was a low-down trick and he said so himself. But he declared it was an ill wind that blew nobody good, and he hinted that maybe in consequence of the trouble she would be better off than if it hadn't happened."

Carl bit his tongue to keep it silent. How he longed to impart to his chum the good tidings that would greet him when he reached home! But he must not spoil Louise's pleasure by telling the story of her good luck for her.

"Oh, somehow things do seem to come round right if you wait long enough," mumbled he.

"So mother says," echoed Hal moodily. "But you get almighty sick of waiting sometimes. Even knowing you were right doesn't put pennies in your pocket." He laughed with a touch of bitterness.

Again Carl was tempted to break the silence and reveal the wonderful secret, and again he clamped his lips together.

Hal would hear the tidings soon enough now and his spirits would soar the higher because of the depths to which they had descended. It was always so. This broad range of mood was one of his chief charms.

Ah, how well he knew his friend and how accurately did he forecast what would happen!

It was not five minutes after the two parted at the corner before Hal Harling came leaping up the McGregors' stairway and gave a loud knock at their door.

"Oh, you old tight-jaw!" announced he, when on entering, he beheld Carl grinning at him from across the room. "You might have put me out of my misery."

The boy laughed.

"It wasn't my secret! I'd have been a cur to butt in on Louise's fun."

"So you would!"

Quietly Mrs. McGregor glanced up from the sea of delicate blue gauze foaming about her.

"A ready tongue is a gift of silver, but a silent one is a treasure of pure gold," observed she quaintly.

CHAPTER VII

THE COMING OF THE FAIRY GODMOTHER

With the Harlings safely out of their difficulties Christmas, as Carl jestingly observed, was free to approach and approach it did with a speed incredible of belief. A big blizzard a week before it, which transformed the suburban districts into a wonderland of beauty, merely worked havoc however in Baileyville, causing muddy streets and slippery pavements, and wrecking the skating in the park.

"Snow doesn't seem to be made for cities," remarked Mrs. McGregor in reply to Carl's lamentations. "It is an old-fashioned institution that belongs to the past. Here in town there is neither a place for it nor does it do an atom of good to anybody unless it is the unemployed who hail the work it brings."

"I hate the snow," wailed Timmie. "It isn't snow, anyway; it's just slush."

"Ah, laddie, you should see one of the snowstorms of the old country!" protested his Scotch mother reminiscently. "Then you would not say you hated the snow. It turned everything it touched white as a Tartary lamb."

"What's a Tartary lamb, Mother?" inquired Tim with interest.

"A Tartary lamb? Ask your big brother; he goes to school."

"I never heard of a Tartary lamb, Ma," flushed Carl.

"Mary had a little lamb," began Nell, who had caught the phrase.

"So she did, darling," laughed her mother as she picked up the child and kissed her, "and its fleece was white as snow, too, for the song says so; but it wasn't a Tartary lamb, dearie. It was just a common one."

"What is a Tartary lamb, anyway, Ma?" Mary demanded.

Mrs. McGregor paused to put a length of silk into her needle.

"Long ago," began she, "before there were ships and trains, to say nothing of automobiles and aeroplanes people had to stay at home in the places where they happened to be born. Of course they could go by coach or on horseback to a near-by city, but they could not go far; nor indeed did they think of going because they did not know there was anywhere to go. Nobody did any traveling in those days and as a result there were no maps or travel books to set you thinking you must pack up your traps to-morrow and start for some place you never had seen. But by and by the compass was invented, larger and better ships came to be built, and men got the idea the world was round instead of flat (as they had at one time supposed), a discovery that comforted vastly the timid souls who had always been afraid of falling off the edge of it. Therefore, when it was at last proved that should you sail far, far away your ship, instead of dropping off into space, would circle the great ball we live on and come home again, some of those who were brave, adventurous, and had money enough set out on voyages to see what there was to be seen in other lands than those they had been brought up in. Frenchmen thought it would be a grand thing to discover new countries for France; Englishmen wanted new territory for England. So it was all over the world. Thus this one and that one began to travel."

"Just as Columbus came to America, Ma," put in Tim.

"Exactly, dear," nodded his mother. "Now you can imagine what a hero such a traveler became; how people admired his daring; and how half of them wished they were going with him and the other half rejoiced that they weren't. And when he came back there was great excitement to hear where he had been and what he had seen! Every word he spoke was passed from mouth to mouth, each person who repeated it adding to the story until it grew like a snowball. And as was inevitable the more raptly the populace listened the more marvelous became the stories."

"Like Jack Murphy when he gets home from the circus," put in Tim.

"Yes, very much like Jack Murphy, I am afraid; only sometimes these travelers really believed the tales they told. Sometimes the stories had been passed on to them by the natives of the strange countries they visited, and how could they know that all which was told them was not true? Such a tale was the legend of the Tartary lamb."

"Tell it to us, Mother," urged Mary.

"Well, it actually isn't much of a story, my dear. You see, when the travelers from England, France, and other western countries went to the East for the first time, they saw cotton growing, or if they did not really see it, they heard there was such a thing. Now cotton was entirely new to the voyagers and it seemed unbelievable that such a plant could be. Some of the eastern natives told the visitors that in each pod grew a little lamb with soft, white fleece. Orientals were very ignorant in those days. The Tartars went even farther and said the lamb bent the stalk he lived on down to the ground and ate all the food within reach; and when he had nibbled up all the grass and roots around him he died, and then it was that people took his fleece and twisted it into thread, which was woven into garments. Thus the legend became established and the belief in the Tartary lamb became so firm that for several hundred years people even in England thought that in the Far East there grew this wonderful plant with a vegetable lamb sprouting from the top of it."

"How silly of them!" sniffed Carl.

"No sillier than lots of the things we now believe, probably," replied his mother. "Aren't we constantly discovering how mistaken some of our cherished beliefs were? That is what progress is. We learn continually to cast aside outgrown notions and adopt wiser and better ones. So it was in the past. The world was very young in those days, you must remember, and people did not know so much about it as we do now. And even we, with all our wisdom, are going to be laughed at years hence, precisely as you are laughing now about those who believed the story of the Tartary lamb. Men are going to say: *'Think of those poor, stupid old things back in nineteen hundred and twenty-three who believed so-and-so! How could they have done it?'*"

Carl was silent.

"When you consider this you will understand how it was that the eager readers of the past devoured with wide-open eyes the tale-telling of Sir John Mandeville; and should you ever read that ancient story, as I hope you will sometime, you will be less surprised to hear that even he declared that he had seen cotton growing and that when the pod of the plant was cut open inside it was a little creature like a lamb. The natives of the East ate both the fruit of the plant and the wee beast, he explained. In fact he said he had eaten the thing himself."

"Why, the very idea!" gasped Mary.

"What a lie!" Carl burst out.

"I'm afraid Sir John was either not very truthful or he had a great imagination," smiled Mrs. McGregor. "Still, you see, he was not alone in his belief about the Tartary lamb. So many other people believed the yarn that he probably thought he was telling the truth. And as for eating it—well, he just had a strain of Jack Murphy in him. Besides, there were no schools in 1322 to teach Sir John Mandeville better. And anyway, who was to contradict the fable? Sir John had been to the East and the other people hadn't. Why shouldn't they believe what he and other travelers told them?"

"He did sort of have them, didn't he?" grinned Carl.

"How long was it before the public stopped believing such a ridiculous story?" demanded Mary.

"About three hundred years," answered her mother. "In the meantime much traveling had been done by the peoples of all nations and learning had made great strides. Scientific men began to whisper there could be no such thing as the lamb of the Tartars; it was not possible. Cotton was merely a plant. You can imagine what discussions such an assertion as that raised. The public had come to like the notion of the Tartary lamb and did not wish to give it up; besides, if the story were all a myth, it put the travelers who had told it in a very bad light, and shook the confidence of readers in some of the other tales they had published. Science always upsets us. None of us like to be jolted out of the beliefs we have been brought up with and exchange them for others, no matter how good the new ones are. So it was in sixteen hundred. The populace resented having the Tartary lamb taken away from them."

Mrs. McGregor laughed.

"It was a pity Sir John Mandeville and the rest did not live long enough to learn how mistaken they had been," mused Mary.

"Poor old Sir John! I guess it was as well for him that he didn't, for in his day he was, you see, quite a celebrity. He might not have relished living to see his fame evaporate. At least he had the courage to make a trip to a strange and distant land, and for that we should respect him since it took nerve to travel in those days. Moreover he did his part and was a link in a civilization that went on after he was gone. So the history of the world is built up. Each generation builds on the blunders of the one before it—or should."

"How queer it makes you feel; and how small!" Mary reflected. "Why?"

"Well, it just seems as if we didn't count for much," sighed the girl.

"On the contrary, dear child, we count for a great deal," instantly retorted her mother. "Each one of us can have a share in the vast plan of the universe and help carry it forward."

"How, Mother?"

"By doing all we can during our lifetime to make the world better," was the answer. "Good men and good women make a good world, don't they? And the better the world the farther ahead will be its civilization. Progress is not all in wonderful discoveries of science, in fine architecture, or in great books; much of it lies in the peoples of the globe learning to live peacefully together and help one another. Kindness to our neighbor, therefore, helps civilization. It cannot avoid doing so if we live it on a large enough scale."

"I never thought of that before," meditated Carl.

"But you can see it is so, laddie," responded his mother. "A lack of kindness and fairness in nations causes wars, and wars put the world backward. It is in the peaceful times that nations grow. You know yourself that you cannot build up anything when somebody else is waiting to knock it down the minute you have it finished. Under such conditions it hardly seems worth while to build at all. So it is with nations the world over. When they are snarling jealously at one another's heels, and coveting what the other possesses, how can progress be made?"

"I suppose when they get mad they forget about the work of the world," Tim announced.

"That is just the trouble," agreed his mother. "Engrossed in their own little squabbles, they lose sight of the splendid big thing they were put here to do. In other words they forget their job, which is to make the world and themselves better."

Slowly she glanced from one earnest face into another.

"Well, I've read you quite a sermon, haven't I?" smiled she. "And it was all because of the Tartary lamb. Now suppose we talk of something else—Christmas. It will be here now before we know it. What shall we do this year? Shall it be a tree? Or shall we hang our stockings, go without a tree, and put the money into a Christmas dinner?"

Inquiringly she studied her children's faces.

"I suppose a tree does cost quite a lot before you are through with it," reflected the prudent Mary.

"And we have the municipal tree in the park, anyway," Carl put in in an attempt to be optimistic.

"But that tree isn't ours, our very own tree," Tim began to wail.

"It is lots bigger than any tree we could have, Timmie," asserted his older brother. "And think of the lights! They are all electric. We couldn't have lights like those here at home."

"I know," grieved Tim. "But it isn't our tree—just ours—in our house."

"A Christmas tree costs ever so much money, Timmie,"

Mary explained gently. "Mother can't buy us a tree always and a dinner, too."

"Oh, I could manage a small tree, perhaps," interrupted Mrs. McGregor, touched at seeing the child so disappointed. "There are little ones at the market."

"But I don't want a little one," objected Tim stubbornly. "I want a big, big Christmas tree."

"Big as the ceiling—big as Mulberry Court," interrupted Martin, extending his chubby arms to their full length.

"I wants a big tree, too," lisped Nell.

Mrs. McGregor sighed to herself. Evidently it was not going to be as easy to coax her flock away from their established traditions as she had at first supposed. Each year she had made a stupendous effort to keep Christmas after the old fashion; and each season the ceremony, before it was over, made appalling inroads on her slender purse. This time it had been her plan to curtail expenses and put what was spent into the more substantial and lasting things. But now as she glanced about her her heart misgave her. Even Carl and Mary, valiantly as they fought for economy, and grown up though they were, could not altogether conceal the fact that they were disappointed; and as for the younger children, they were on the brink of tears.

"Well, we won't decide to-day," announced their mother diplomatically. "We will think it over until to-morrow. By that time perhaps some way can be found——"

A knock at the door interrupted her.

"Run to the door like a good boy, Timmie," said she. "Very likely it's the boy from the corner grocery with the bundles of wood I ordered."

Tim rose with importance. Visitors to the fifth floor of

Mulberry Court were so few that to admit even so prosaic a one as the grocer's boy never ceased to thrill him.

To-day, however, it was not the grocer's boy who stood peering at him from the dim hallway. In fact, it was no one he had ever seen before. A little old man stood there, a man with ruddy cheeks, a stern mouth, and blue eyes whose sharpness was softened by a moist, far-away expression. From beneath a nautical blue cap strayed a wisp or two of white hair. Other-wise, he was buttoned to his chin in a great coat, fastened with imposing brass buttons, dulled by much fingering.

Apprehensive at the sight, Tim backed into the room. Brass buttons, in his limited experience, meant either firemen or policemen and either of these dignitaries was equally terrifying.

"You don't know your Uncle Frederick, do you, sonny?" observed the stranger.

The voice, more than the words, brought Mrs. McGregor to her feet in an instant, and what a rush she made for the door! Gauze, spangles, scissors, and spool flew in all directions and the children, deciding that some unprecedented evil had befallen, stampeded after her.

Open-mouthed, they watched, while in the arms of the little old gentleman she laughed, cried, and uttered broken nothings quite unintelligible to anybody.

"Who ever would have thought to see you, Frederick!" gasped she at last, as wiping her eyes on the corner of her apron she dragged her visitor into the room. "Children, come here one by one and speak to your Uncle James Frederick Dillingham. This is Carl, the oldest one—a good boy as ever lived (if he is always tearing his clothes). The next is Mary; she's going on thirteen and is quite a little housekeeper even now. Timmie, who let you in, is nine. And here are Martin and Nell—the mites! James

Frederick is asleep but when you see him you'll see the finest baby you ever set your two eyes on. Kiss your uncle, children. You know it's him you have to thank for many, many things."

Slowly the children advanced, wonder (and if the truth must be told) no small measure of chagrin in their crestfallen countenances.

Was this apparition the fairy prince of their imaginings—this little gray man with his long coat and oilskin bundle? Why, he might be Mike Carrigan, the butcher; or Davie Ryan, the proprietor of the fruit stand, for anything his appearance denoted. Their dreams were in the dust. Still, youth is hopeful and they did not quite let go the expectation that when the long coat that disguised him had been removed and the magic bundle opened Uncle Frederick Dillingham would issue forth in a garb startling, resplendent, and more in accordance with their mental pictures of him. But to their profound disappointment, when the great coat was tossed aside, it concealed no ermine-robed hero; nor was there crown or scepter in the bundle. Instead there stood in their midst a very plain, kindly little man arrayed in a shiny suit of blue serge that was almost shabby. The buttons, to be sure, had anchors on them; but they were dim, lusterless old anchors that looked as if they had been sunk in the depths of the sea until their golden glory had been tarnished by the washings of a million waves.

Nell eyed him and at length began to cry.

"Policeman!" she whimpered, hiding her face in her mother's skirt.

"Hush, girlie! Don't be silly," protested Mrs. McGregor hurriedly. "Your uncle is no policeman, though he may get one if you don't stop that noise."

At that the little old man laughed a hearty, ringing laugh, so good to hear that in spite of themselves the whole family joined in it. After that, everything was easy. Uncle James Frederick Dillingham tucked his coat, cap, and bundle away in a corner and allowed his sister to seat him in the rocking-chair before the stove.

"Put another shovelful of coal on the fire, Carl," said she briskly. "And Mary, do you slip out to the market and fetch home a beefsteak and some onions. You were ever fond of a steak smothered in onions, Frederick. Timmie, you shall set the table with a place for your uncle Frederick at the head, remember. And Nell, trot to the shed, darling, and bring mother a nice lot of potatoes. Go softly so not to waken James Frederick."

Promptly her host sprang to obey her.

"Well, well, Brother," murmured she, "I've scarcely got my breath yet. I never was so surprised in all my born days as to see you standing there on the mat! Wherever did you come from? We've not heard from you for weeks and I had begun to fear something might have gone amiss."

Captain Dillingham patted her hand with his horny one.

"We had a long trip home, Nellie, because of strong head winds," explained he. "Then, too, there were ports to stop at and cargo to unload. Add to this a fracas with the engine and you'll readily understand why I had only scant time for letter writing. I never was any too good at it, at best, you know."

"Men never are," returned Mrs. McGregor cheerily over her shoulder as she hustled out of the pantry with a clean tablecloth. "But it matters not now; the ship is safe in port and you are here in time for Christmas—a miracle that's never happened before in all my memory."

"But——," began her brother doubtfully.

"But what? Surely you're not going to say you are putting

straight off to-morrow for India or some other heathen spot! No shipowners would be so heartless as to ask you to do that. Besides, very like the *Charlotte* must need repairing after such a stiff trip. Oughtn't her seams to be caulked or something?"

Captain Dillingham's eyes twinkled and the corners of his mouth curved upward.

"You're quite knowing in nautical matters, Nellie," observed he with amusement. "Aye, the *Charlotte* will have to lay to and be overhauled some. She had a tough voyage. Still, she don't mind it much. She's a thoroughbred that takes what comes without whimpering. That's the lady of her. I never have to offer excuses or apologies for her—no, siree! Tell her what you want done and you can count on her doing it every time."

"I'm sorry you didn't have a better voyage home," ventured his sister.

"Oh, the voyage was all right enough. You can't expect a marble floor to sail on in December. Indeed a trip such as that would be almost too tame for me. I like the kick of the sea. Still, heavy winds that hold you back all the way over as these held us, are trying. You make but slow progress against them. Nevertheless the *Charlotte* put up a stiff fight and don't you forget it."

"Had you any storms this trip?"

"Storms? Oh, I believe we did strike a gale or two, now I come to think of it. I recall there was a nasty typhoon in the Indian Ocean that kept us busy for a while. But such happenings are all in the day's work and after they are over are forgotten."

Carl, busy at his task of slicing the bread, gasped. Gales and typhoons! And the Indian Ocean to boot! And his uncle mentioned them all as if they were no more than flies on the wall. He had seen the Indian Ocean on the map—an area of blue edged about with patches of pink, green, and yellow; but he certainly had never expected to meet in the flesh anybody who had sailed its waters.

Uncle Frederick Dillingham suddenly began to take on in his eyes an aspect quite new; an aspect so alluring that when contrasted with the myth of purple and ermine the latter tradition shriveled into something very minor in importance. Was not the master of a ship a far more intriguing character than a dull old king who did nothing but sit on a crimson velvet throne and wave a scepter?

"You'll have much to tell us, Frederick," declared Mrs. McGregor, putting the potatoes into the oven. "The children know little of foreign lands. Nor do I know as much of them as I would. 'Twill be grand to hear where you've been and what you've seen."

"Did you go to China, Uncle Frederick?" Carl inquired timidly.

"Aye! And to India and Japan, laddie."

The boy's eyes glowed with excitement.

"Oh, wouldn't I like to sail on a big ship to some place that was different from Mulberry Court!" cried he.

"The places I've been in lately were certainly different from Mulberry Court!" sighed Captain Dillingham. "And perhaps had you seen them you would be as glad as I am to be at Mulberry Court."

"Maybe! I'd like a peep at something else, though."

"Maybe some day you'll be having it," returned the sea captain jocosely. "Who knows! I may be taking you to India with me when you're older."

"*Frederick!*" came from Mrs. McGregor in a horrified tone.

"You wouldn't like to see the shaver starting off for India, Nellie? And why not?" laughed her brother. "India is a fine country. Besides, traveling the world is a great way to study its geography. I'll be willing to wager, now, that not one of these older children, though they have been to school since they were knee high, could tell me offhand where the Suez Canal is."

Consternation greeted the assertion and there was dead silence.

"There! What did I tell you?" returned Captain Dillingham triumphantly. "And should I try them on the Bay of Biscay or the Ganges it would be no better."

The stillness was oppressive.

"Aren't there—didn't I read somewhere that there are crocodiles in the Ganges?" Carl managed to stammer.

His uncle chuckled.

"There's hope for you, son," he answered. "To know there are crocodiles in the Ganges is something. Perhaps I shall make a tourist of you yet. But you will have to know a little more about this globe of ours before I can do it, I'm afraid."

"I hate geography," announced Tim, who had been listening and now with disconcerting frankness proclaimed his aversion in no uncertain terms. "All it is is little squares of color."

Captain Dillingham glanced toward his sister and met her wry smile.

"That's what books do for you," acclaimed he. "They make the romance of the Orient nothing but patchwork." Then to Tim he continued, "I can teach you better geography than that, laddie. Countries aren't just little pieces of pink, yellow, or blue paper laid together. They are people, rivers, mountains; tea, sugar, and cotton; ivory, elephants, and carved temples."

The children had drawn closer around his knee.

"Tell us about the elephants," pleaded Tim, with shining eyes.

"There, you see! You are begging already for a lesson in geography—much as you dislike it!" teased his uncle.

"There can be no geography lessons now," objected Mrs. McGregor. "The steak is done and mustn't be spoiled with waiting. Show your uncle where to sit, Mary. And, Timmie, bring the salt. It's been forgotten. You'll have to bring a chair from my room, Martin. Remember James Frederick and go on your toes."

"Now, Frederick," smiled his sister mischievously, "admit that even in India you've seen nothing better than this beefsteak."

"'Twill take no coaxing to make me admit that, my dear," returned Captain Dillingham. "Not all the sultans of the east could produce a dish as royal as this one."

CHAPTER VIII

THE ROMANCE OF COTTON

From the moment of Uncle James Frederick Dillingham's arrival there began for the McGregor children an era of delight. The newly found relative, they soon discovered, was not only all they had pictured, but more—far more!

He did not, it is true, actually live at Mulberry Court, for because of the crowded conditions of the McGregor home he took a room near-by; nevertheless he might as well have lived there for he only used his own room to sleep in and stow away his luggage. Each morning just before breakfast his step would be heard on the stairs and off would race the children in merry rivalry to see who would reach the door first and have the honor of admitting him. Once inside the cosy kitchen he made it his headquarters and it did not take long to find out that he was a valuable asset there.

For example who could fry fish so deliciously as he? And who could make such chowder? And as for washing dishes and wiping them he was quicker than any of the young folks. To behold an officer in gold braid presiding at the dishpan at first caused a protest from Mrs. McGregor; but when the little old man asserted that it was a treat to be inside a home and handle a mop and soap-shaker what could one say? So he mixed the foaming suds and dabbled in them up to his elbows, and when his sister witnessed the general frolic into which his leadership suddenly transformed the dishwashing she no longer objected. The center of an admiring group of youngsters Uncle Frederick scrubbed pots and pans until they shone like mirrors, and all to a chain of the most wonderful stories.

What marvel that there were quarrels as to who should help him and actual bribes offered for the coveted pleasure? The children's chatter never tired him. On the contrary he was in his element when they swarmed about his chair and perched on his knee. As for his namesake, James Frederick, there was not another such baby to be found in all the world, he declared. Often he would sit with the little fellow in his arms, crooning to him fragments of old sea chanties whose refrains were haunting to hear. Or he wheeled the baby out with as much pride as if he were treading the decks of the *Charlotte*.

To see him one would have imagined that he had always lived at Mulberry Court. How naturally, for example, he wandered into the market, bringing back with him mysterious bundles which on being opened disclosed lamb chops, sweet potatoes, and oranges. And what a feast big and little McGregors had when such parcels made their advent in the kitchen! Or he would venture into the shopping district and appear with his pockets bulging with rubbers, mittens, and caps. Oh, there never was such an uncle! His purse seemed lined with gold; or if it were not lined with this precious metal at least the supply of pennies it contained was unending.

And not only was there one of these shiny pennies for each child in the family but before long the train of benefactions lengthened until there was scarce a boy or girl to be found in all Mulberry Court who did not have tucked away in his mitten a golden disc with the shining face of Abraham Lincoln upon it.

So it was that he became uncle not alone to the wee McGregors but to the community as well.

Now of course it followed that such a visitor could not be more than a short cycle of hours in the neighborhood without making the acquaintance of the Harlings, and running in to amuse the shut-ins with his tales of foreign lands. For he was a rare story-teller, was Uncle Frederick. Never was there a better. And with running here and running there was it to be wondered at that he found himself as busy if not busier than he had been when aboard the *Charlotte*—a very lucky thing too, for he confided that he always got fidgety for his ship if he was idle when on shore.

Now he had no chance to become nervous or fretful. Much travel had rendered it easy for him to establish contacts with persons. In consequence all types of human beings interested him and with a charm quite his own he swept aside the preliminaries and by simple and direct methods made straight for the hearts of those he met. He reached them, too—there was no doubt about that. Had he chosen he could have astounded Mulberry Court with all he knew about Julie O'Dowd, the Murphys, and the Sullivans. Why, he even knew all about Davis and Coulter's mills before he had been in Baileyville twenty-four hours!

Now this delightful relative could not but increase in the community the prestige of the McGregor family. To have a connection so popular, traveled, and prosperous—a man of rank, and adorned with brass buttons, what a luster all this shed over the inhabitants of the fifth floor of Mulberry Court! Carl, Mary, Tim, Martin, were no longer rated as little street Arabs; suddenly they became the nieces, nephews (probably the heirs) of Captain James Frederick Dillingham who commanded the *Charlotte* and had sailed to every port under the sun. How the neighbors gossiped, congratulating themselves that they had discovered Mrs. McGregor's virtues in time to be included in her circle of acquaintances! Oh, they had always known she was a lady! Wasn't her ancestry stamped upon her very face?

As for the Captain himself, his career, when contrasted with the humdrum life of Mulberry Court, was like that of a returned Columbus. How could he fail to be enveloped in a halo of fascination? For Mulberry Court was dingy and dull. Probably not one of its toiling throng was destined ever to see much beyond the city's muddy streets, crowded sidewalks, cheap shops, and seething tenements. But at least, even right here in Baileyville, it was possible to glimpse through other eyes the wonders denied them.

Therefore when Captain Dillingham came to call one did the next best thing to really going to India—one went there by proxy and saw in imagination white-turbaned natives, resplendent temples, sun-flooded tropics arched by turquoise skies. Even the Murphys could do that, and without it costing them a cent, either. The Captain told Julie O'Dowd stories of China while she ironed Joey's dresses, and the tediousness of the task was forgotten in the enchantment of the tale. As for Grandfather Harling, after the stranger's first visit he strained his ears for a second, and when with a cheery "Ahoy!" the knob turned and the small gray man entered, it seemed as if the very sunlight came with him. And Mrs. Harling welcomed his coming too for even the men's talk of cargoes, commerce, shipping, and stevedores had its lure for her.

In fact, all the neighborhood agreed that the dapper little captain "had a way with him."

"Why, he could actually talk about dried codfish, I do believe, and make you think there was nothing on earth like it!" exclaimed

Julie O'Dowd to Mrs. Murphy. "I never saw such a man! And so kind withal. Simple as a child, too. You don't catch him prating about his doings. Why, Mike Sullivan who went once to New York talked more about it than does this critter all his circlings of the globe."

Aye, the Captain was modest. Everybody agreed to that. Nevertheless he certainly had at his tongue's end an astonishing amount of information which came hither when occasion arose for him to use it.

Carl had an illustration of that one day when he chanced to drop a remark about the Tartary lamb.

"Tartary lamb, eh!" commented his uncle, catching up the phrase quickly. "And how, pray, did you hear of the Tartary lamb?"

"Mother told us."

"A funny idea, wasn't it?" Uncle Frederick spoke as if Tartary lambs were topics of everyday conversation. "And yet no stranger than some of the notions we hold now, I imagine. We do not know all there is to be known ourselves—not by a good sight—even though we do think ourselves very up-to-date. With all the learning the ages have rolled up handed to us in a bundle we should blush were we not better informed than poor Sir John Mandeville, who had no books to speak of. Had he been able to read Herodotus, for example, he would then have learned from that Greek writer who lived so many centuries ago that there was in India a wild tree having for its fruit fleeces finer than those of sheep; and that the natives spun cloth out of them and made clothing for themselves. Herodotus tells many other interesting facts about cotton and its uses, too. A present, he remarks, sent to the king of Egypt, was packed in cotton so that it would not get broken. That sounds natural, doesn't it? He even makes our clever inventor, Eli Whitney, appear unoriginal by describing a Greek machine that separated cotton seeds from the fiber."

"Then the cotton gin wasn't new, after all," frowned Carl.

"The idea of it was not new, no; but the device Whitney and his friend Mr. Miller produced was a fresh method for getting this age-old result. Up to 1760 the same primitive ginning machine was used in England as had been used in India for many, many years. Think of that! But as civilization grew and people not only wove more cloth but made an increasing variety of kinds the demand for material to make it increased. And old Herodotus is by no means the only early historian to mention cotton. Other writers went into even more details than he, describing the plant, its leaves and blossoms, and telling how it was set out in rows. Apparently as long ago as 519 B.C. the Persians were spinning and weaving cloth and dyeing it all sorts of colors, using for the purpose the leaves and roots of tropical plants. It therefore followed that when the officers of Emperor Alexander's army returned from the East they brought back to Greece tales of the cotton plant, and Greeks and Romans alike began to use the material for awnings much as we do now."

"How funny!" smiled Carl. "I'll bet they were glad to have something to shade them from the sun. I shouldn't relish spending the summer in Greece or Italy."

"I guess you wouldn't. Baileyville may be hot in July but it is nothing to what Rome must have been. The stone seats of the Forum were like stove covers; and because the rich old Romans enjoyed comfort quite as much as anybody else, lengths of cotton cloth were stretched across certain parts of the structure to shade it. Even your friend Julius Cæsar was not so toughened by battle that he fancied having the hot sun beat down on his head; he therefore ordered a screening of cloth to be extended from the top of his house to that of the Capitoline Hill so when he rode hither he could be cool and sheltered. Oh, the Romans knew a good thing when they saw it—never fear! In the meantime Greeks and Romans alike were using the newly discovered material for tents, sails, and gay-colored coverlets."

"Didn't cotton grow in any other country beside India, Uncle Frederick?" interrogated Mary.

"We do not really know about that," was her uncle's reply. "Certainly it was found in other places—Egypt, Africa, Mexico, and America; but whether it was native to these lands or had been transplanted to them it is impossible to say. We do know, however, that the ancient Egyptians depended chiefly on flax for their cloth and imported cotton from other countries, so although the plant did grow there they could not have had much of it. The little they had was cultivated, I believe, almost entirely as a shrub and used merely for decoration."

"But loads of cotton come from Egypt now," declared Carl. "The teacher told us so."

"Indeed it does," nodded Captain Dillingham. "I have brought many a bale of it back in my ship, so I know."

"Really!" ejaculated his listeners.

"Yes; Egypt, India, and the United States are the great cotton-producing countries of the world. India comes first on the list; then we ourselves, with our vast southern crops; then Egypt. And it is because India raises such great quantities of cotton and is obliged to ship it to England for manufacture afterward buying it back again—that Gandhi and his followers who are eager for India to be independent of England are raising little patches of cotton, weaving their own cloth on hand looms, and refusing to purchase that of English make. It certainly seems fair enough that the wealth derived from this crop should remain in India and not be spent for things the people of India do not like. However, all that is too big a question for you and me."

"Did you ever see cotton growing, Uncle Frederick?" asked Tim, who had drawn near.

"Oh, often, sonny. As a general thing the plant is like a Christmas tree in shape. The perennial plants, or those that come up every year, frequently grow to be six or eight feet tall; but the annual ones remain little three or four-foot bushes. Still each grows into pyramid form, having the wider branches at the bottom. The leaves are not unlike the lilac; and there is a deep, cup-shaped pod having points that turn up like fingers and hold the cotton in tightly. But no matter whether perennial or annual, the cotton plant must have a hot, humid climate to thrive, and if the land is not naturally moist it must be irrigated as it is in Egypt."

"I thought things like cotton just grew wild, Uncle Frederick," said Tim.

"No, indeed," laughed his uncle. "You cannot gather big crops of anything unless you are willing to work for them. The Lord does not mean to make life too easy for us. He gives us all these things and then He has done His part; we must do the rest. The world is a place of opportunities, that is all. If we are too lazy to take them, or too stupid, it is our own fault. Many a man gets nowhere because he fails to grasp this idea. So, sonny, you do not get your cotton all grown for you, and with the seeds picked out. You are given the root and if you wish a big cotton crop you must plant seeds, or better yet set out cuttings, cultivate and care for the plants. Every minute your mind must be on the thing you are trying to raise. You must watch, for instance, for pests of insects; diseases that will spoil your plants; blights caused by fungi; and above all for sudden changes in the weather. Should it turn scorching hot just when your cotton shoots are up and beginning to spread their roots the result will be fatal. Or an early frost will work ruin. Sometimes, you know, we have a spell of hot weather in the late winter that fools the growing things into thinking spring has come, and the poor misguided plants begin to put out their leaves. Then, like a mischievous joker, old Winter comes back and nips the trusting little creatures. Cotton doesn't fancy that sort of joke. Nor does it like too much wet weather, for then the cotton gets damp and sodden and cannot be picked. Should it be gathered in this condition it would mold and mildew, and become a wreck."

"It sounds to me as if cotton raising was pretty hard work," sighed Tim.

"Oh, no harder than are most other things, Timmie," returned Uncle Frederick. "Generally speaking cotton plants sail along safely enough unless a pest attacks them. That is their greatest menace. When a pest descends on the crop the grower does lose courage, I can tell you. It is queer to think what damage a crowd of tiny insects can do, isn't it? Some of them will bore through the pods as if in pure spite and spoil the cotton fiber at the time it is just beginning to form—a detestable trick! Others, fattening on the tender green leaves near the top of the plant, will turn into caterpillars, creep down the stalk, and devour every leaf as they go along. This leaves the roots of the plant unprotected from the sun and speedily every particle of moisture on which the growth is so dependent is dried up. So the plants shrivel and die. Then there are beetles, locusts, grasshoppers, and all the rest of the army of trouble-makers who wait to steal a march on the unwatchful planter. All these rebels must be kept their distance if you would harvest a big cotton crop."

"I guess I never would have any cotton," remarked the disheartened Tim.

"Oh, yes, you would, son," laughed his uncle. "Surely you wouldn't let yourself be beaten by a lot of bugs and worms, would you? Should you live in a climate where cotton could be raised you would pitch in, fight the pests, and be as proud of your snowy field as many another man is. For when the pods are ready for gathering there is no prettier sight. It is like a huge bowl of popcorn."

"I'd like to see a cotton field," ventured Mary.

"You'd have to go to India, the southern part of your own country, Australia, Brazil, Egypt, or the South Sea Islands then," Captain Dillingham responded. "That is, if you wanted to see the best of it—that which is strongest of fiber."

"But isn't cotton all alike?" queried the girl, with parted lips.

"No, indeed, child! There are many different kinds of cotton. Some have seeds of one color, some of another; some seeds come out easily, some do not; some cotton is strong fibered, some is weak and snaps at a touch; some has long fibers and some short. Each variety has its name and is peculiar to a given country."

"Oh!" came in chorus from his audience.

"For instance, the most delicate or fine quality of thread is produced from the Sea Island cotton, and usually this type is quite expensive; it has so many seeds and they take up so much room in the pod that after they have been removed only a small quantity of cotton remains and that makes it costly. Almost every other kind gives more lint (or picked cotton) than does this variety. The Egyptian cotton is somewhat on this same order. India, China, Arabia, Persia, Asia Minor, Africa, and the Coromandel Coast all have a common type of plant which probably first grew in the latter place and was transplanted from there to the other countries.

"In Cuba a sort of cotton vine is found that has very large pods and a great number of seeds. Some of the fibers of this plant are long and some short. It is not a very good kind of cotton to cultivate because the long fibers get tangled up with the seeds and often break when being separated. Moreover the short fibers are all mixed in with the long.

"This gives you some notion of the different species of cotton. Were I to tell you of all the kinds you would be tired hearing about them. I myself get interested because I carry so much cotton in my ship—bales upon bales of it. Sometimes I take cotton out from America to countries that either do not have any, or do not have as much as they want; sometimes I bring back here varieties that we cannot raise in the South."

"What kind of cotton do we raise in the United States?" Mary asked.

"The bulk of our cotton is long-stapled and is called Georgian Upland," was the response. "The whole plant is rough and hairy—leaf, branch, and pod. Some persons think that originally it came from Mexico. However that may be, here it is, and although we raise some little of other sorts we have far more of this than anything else. We can thank it, too, for much of the wealth of this country of ours for Texas, Georgia, Alabama, North and South Carolina, Mississippi, Louisiana and Arkansas are all big cotton-growing States. Florida, Tennessee, Indian Territory, Missouri, Virginia, Kentucky, Kansas, and Oklahoma also lie in the cotton belt and ship substantial crops."

The little man rose.

"I could go on talking cotton forever," jested he. "Think of a sacred cotton tree often as high as twenty feet, growing along the coast of the Indian Ocean, the cotton from which is used only for weaving cloth for the turbans of Hindoo priests! And think of still another exquisitely fine Indian cotton called Dacca cotton that is spun and woven into fragile oriental muslins and Madras Long Cloth. It almost makes your mouth water to grow cotton, doesn't it?"

"Well, at least you can go and see it grown, Uncle Frederick, and that is more than we can do," piped Tim.

"True, sonny," nodded the captain. "But still you who stay at home and do not see it grown have your share in its benefits. You wear, use, and eat cotton products."

"How?" questioned the wondering Tim.

"Don't you have cotton cloth for clothing, bedding, and no end of other comforts? Of course you do."

"But—eating cotton———" faltered Tim. "I don't do that."

"There are medicines made from the cotton root; cottonseed oil for cooking and to use on salads, you may not be aware, comes from the meaty kernel inside the cotton seed."

"I didn't know that," Tim answered.

"Oh, cotton has many by-products," returned his uncle. "The lint that cannot be used for spinning is made into cotton wadding to pad quilts, skirts, and coat linings; and cotton waste is excellent for cleaning machinery. Ripe cotton fiber furnishes an almost pure cellulose, too."

"Cotton certainly seems to do its part in the world," Mary murmured thoughtfully. "But I'm not sure," added she, with a mischievous little smile, "that I know just what cellulose is."

CHAPTER IX

NORTH AND SOUTH

Where do you and the Charlotte go when you leave here, Frederick?" his sister inquired as the family sat at breakfast the next morning.

"New Orleans, I suppose; we touch there for a cargo of cotton," was the reply.

"Then you'll see the crop gathered, won't you, Uncle Frederick?" Mary put in.

"Hardly that, lassie," replied her uncle kindly. "All the work will be done before I arrive. However, I shall not mind that for I have seen southern cotton fields in their prime before now."

"It grows everywhere in the South, doesn't it?" Mary ventured.

"One could hardly say that, my dear," Captain Dillingham responded with a mild shake of his head. "On the contrary the cotton belt of the United States is comparatively small considering the vast crops it yields."

"Why don't they make it bigger and plant more cotton?" questioned Tim.

"Cotton, as I told you, sonny, has its own ideas as to where it will grow. Let it be planted farther north than forty-five degrees and it will only thrive under glass; or try to cultivate it farther south than the thirty-five degree line and it will also balk. This, you see, leaves a rather narrow zone that answers its demands in the way of temperature and soil. For the kind of soil cotton likes has to be considered also. If the land is too sandy the moisture will soon dry up and the plants shrivel; or if there is an undue proportion of clay the excess moisture will not drain off and the plants will run to wood and leaves. Therefore you have the problem of getting the right proportions of clay, loam and sand in a climate where the temperature holds practically even."

"Why, I shouldn't think any spot on earth would fill that bill," grinned Carl.

"We do succeed in getting just such areas, however," returned Captain Dillingham. "North and South Carolina, Georgia, Alabama, Louisiana, Texas, Arkansas, Florida, Tennessee, Indian Territory, Missouri, Virginia, Kentucky, Kansas, and Oklahoma all contrive to answer the requirements to a greater or less degree. These States boast soils that are blends of clay, sand, and loam in the desired proportions; and while some of them are better than others both soil and temperature are such that cotton can be grown in them. Given these two assets the rest of the conundrum is up to the planter."

"I should think most of it was answered for him when he has these two important factors," Mrs. McGregor asserted.

"But to have climate and land is not enough," protested her brother. "Once he possesses the land the owner must take care of it. It cannot be allowed to run out but must be plowed up, fertilized, and the crop tended like any other farm product. Before cotton growers realized this, not much attention was paid to these laws and in consequence the crop of many a southern plantation suffered. Now cotton-raising is done far more scientifically. The old stalks are gathered and destroyed; the land is plowed and fertilized, and afterward seed-planting machines go up and down the rows, scattering five or six seeds into each hole, with a space of not more than a foot between the holes. Then the seeds are covered over lightly and left to sprout."

"How long is it before they come up?" interrogated Carl.

"About ten or twelve days," was the reply. "A couple of days later the first leaf appears and then trouble begins. April sees the Carolina planters thinning their shoots in order to have sturdy plants from which to select the ones eventually allowed to grow. States farther south get at the task earlier. After the thinning process is over the plants are hilled up like potatoes and the spaces between the rows, where the last season's crop previously grew, is plowed to keep the soil open and free for drainage. Men afterward travel through the open rows hoeing up the loose soil and heaping it around the young plants to strengthen and protect them; then, since nothing more can be done immediately everybody takes a rest and waits."

"Then what happens?" piped Tim.

"Oh, after a time the same process is repeated. The earth by this time has become crusted over and must be opened up again; the hauling, too, takes place once more. Hauling is the name given to bedding up the plants with loose earth. Often there are four or five *haulings*. By July the plants have grown sufficiently to show which one in each hill is to be the most thrifty and this one is left to grow while the other shoots are pulled up. After that, given sunny days and occasional light showers, the crop should prosper. Should there, however, be too much heat, or too great a quantity of rain, things will not move so successfully."

"How long does cotton have to grow before it is ready for picking?" asked Carl.

"The plants bloom approximately the middle of June—sometimes earlier, sometimes later, according to the climates of the various States. Two months after that the crop is ready to be gathered. You must not, however, run away with the notion that cotton-picking is a hurried process. Often it goes on from the end of August until into November or December. It is a long-drawn-out, tedious, monotonous task. Whole families join in the harvesting for since there is always some low and some tall cotton (some annual and some perennial varieties) the children can share with their elders in the work and thus earn quite a sum of money. In fact, in the old days before child labor laws protected the kiddies, and while cotton-picking was done by slaves, many a poor little mite toiled cruelly long in the fields. Even the older negroes were driven with whips and compelled to keep at work until utterly exhausted."

His audience gasped.

"Yes," nodded their uncle, "I am afraid that urged forward by the desire to garner a big crop before rain should fall and spoil it, the cotton growers practiced much cruelty. No doubt, too, the same tyranny reigned in India. Wherever work must be done by hand and labor is cheap and plentiful, human beings come to be classed to a great extent as machines. Plantation owners become so interested in the money they are to make that they forget everything else. Of course labor was never as cheap in our Southern States even during slave days as in India and therefore until the advent of the cotton gin, cotton was not one of our valuable crops."

"You mean because the seeds had to be picked out by hand?" Carl said.

"Yes. There was, to be sure, the primitive kind of gin resorted to in India for cleaning certain black-seed varieties. Two kinds of this black-seed, or long-stapled cotton, grew in the Sea Islands and along the coast from Delaware to Georgia; but it could not be made to thrive away from the moist ocean climate. Hence on inland plantations a different and more vigorous variety of plant (one having green seeds and short staples) was propagated. This kind was known as Upland cotton. It was a troublesome product for the planters, I assure you, for its many seeds clung so tightly to the lint that it was almost out of the question to remove them. The simple little gin copied from India and successfully used on the black seed variety was entirely impracticable on this Upland growth since it tore the fibers all to bits."

"They did need a cotton gin, didn't they!" Carl ejaculated.

"Very badly, indeed," agreed Captain Dillingham. "Well, the only substitute for machinery was fingers; and when I tell you that it often took an entire day to get out of a three-pound batch of cotton a pound or so that was clear of seeds you will understand what a slow process it was."

"At that rate I shouldn't think it would have paid anybody to raise cotton," sniffed Carl.

"It didn't," returned his uncle. "Moreover it rendered the product very expensive, for it required a great number of slaves to clean any considerable quantity of cotton. I often think of the toil and misery that went into the cotton-growing of those slavery days. After working for a long stretch of hours in the blazing sun the negroes came in at night worn out. But were they allowed to rest? Perhaps some of them who had considerate owners were; but many, many others less fortunate were set to picking out seeds and lest they fall asleep at their task overseers prodded them with whips."

"Gee!"

"That was slavery, son," declared Captain Dillingham. "Do you wonder that Abraham Lincoln thought it would be worth even a war to rid this country of such an evil? Understand, I am not condemning all slave owners. Undoubtedly there were kind and humane ones just as there are to this day employers who are fair with their help. But urged on by commercial greed the temptation of the planters was to force the slaves to do more than was right, and as a result a great deal of cruelty was practiced. Had the primitive method of picking cotton by hand continued it is probable that slavery might have died a natural death without recourse to war, for many of the Southerners were reaching a point where the returns from cotton and tobacco were not sufficient to feed the army of slaves that swarmed over the plantations. To use a common phrase the slaves were eating their heads off. It was just at this juncture, however, that Eli Whitney came along with his cotton gin and in a twinkling the South became revolutionized and the problem of the legion of idle, profitless slaves was settled. They would now be idle and profitless no longer. Vast quantities of cotton could henceforth be planted and the negroes could cultivate and gather it. With Eli Whitney's gin to do the slow and hindering part of the process cotton-raising could be made a paying industry."

"Mr. Whitney bobbed up in the very nick of time, didn't he?" smiled Mary.

"For the financial prosperity of the South he did," her uncle responded. "But to the welfare of the negroes his advent was a fatal stroke. Slaves immediately were more in demand than they ever had been before. No mechanical device could take their place. Cotton must be planted, cultivated, and harvested by hand and the larger the cotton fields became, the harder the slaves were worked. The cotton crop became the staple product of the South. Many a Southerner who took up arms against the Union did so because he honestly believed that to free the slaves would mean the economic ruin of his section of the country."

"I never thought of that side of the question before," Mrs. McGregor murmured thoughtfully.

"Nor I," rejoined Carl.

"Nevertheless it is a fact none of us here in the North should forget," continued Captain Dillingham. "To the southern planter our point of view appeared unfair and grossly one-sided. It was easy enough for the North to say the slaves should be freed. They had no cotton fields and their prosperity was not dependent on the negroes. But to let the slaves go meant ruin for the South. It was not alone, you see, that their owners wished the profit derived from buying and selling them; they needed them to work. Never had the South had such an opportunity to coin wealth as that now opening. What wonder its residents were angry at having this dazzling prospect for fortune-making snatched away? Remember and take these facts into consideration when you think harshly of those who took up arms to defend slavery."

There was an instant's pause.

"Of course, however, none of this justifies slavery or makes it more right. The entire principle of it was wrong; it was un-Christian, unjust, and cruel, and the only honorable thing to do was to bring it to an end in this country. But that is another story altogether. What we are talking about now is the cotton itself; and to get a big view of this subject it is well to consider what was happening in the world just at this time, and why cotton was such a desirable commodity.

"Over across the ocean James Watts's steam engine, combined with the flying shuttle of John Kay, the spinning jenny of Hargreaves, the water-frame of Arkwright, and the self-acting loom of Crompton, was working as great a revolution in England's cloth-making industry as Eli Whitney's cotton gin had done in the South. In other words the hand loom had been supplanted by the more modern device of the steam-driven spinning mill. This meant that in future cloth would no longer be made in small quantities in the homes, women of the families spinning the thread and weaving it whenever they could steal a bit of time from other household duties. No! Cloth was to be made in factories on a much larger scale, and sold to the public."

"No wonder the fact set everybody to raising cotton!" declared Mrs. McGregor.

"No wonder indeed!" nodded her brother. "From a vintage so small that even President Jefferson scarcely knew America had a cotton crop at all this product of the South leaped forward by bounds. The year preceding Eli Whitney's invention the United States exported less than one hundred and forty thousand bales; but the year afterward the shipment had soared to nearly half a million. The following year it was a million and a half; the year after that six million."

"Gee whizz!" commented Carl. "That was some record, wasn't it?"

"Rather!" agreed his uncle.

"How much do we export now, Uncle Frederick?" Mary asked.

"From nine to twelve million bales of five-hundred pounds each are raised annually in the South," returned Captain Dillingham. "Of this about ninety per cent is Upland cotton, the green seeds of which have to be taken out by a gin similar to the one Eli Whitney invented. Approximately about half this vast crop is exported."

"I had no idea we raised so much cotton," mused Carl.

"We raise quantities of it, son," Uncle Frederick said. "Now you can understand better why the South was so resentful at being compelled to free the slaves. With cotton so much in demand the prices of slaves had greatly increased. The planters had untold wealth almost within their grasp. It was all very well for the North to assert that slavery was a barbarous practise. Who was to tend the cotton fields when the slaves were gone?"

"The South did have something on its side, didn't it?" Mary ventured.

"A great deal, when once you put yourself in the Southerner's place. We in the North are liable to emphasize only the cruelty of slavery and are often unable to understand how enlightened and Christian men could keep slaves and fight to keep them. You see there were reasons."

Mary nodded.

"Of course, as I said before, all the cotton-raising in the world could not make the thing right. It was wrong from start to finish. Nevertheless it does explain why some of our people felt the freeing of the slaves so unjust and such a blow to their prosperity that they threatened secession from the Union."

"And it was because Abraham Lincoln would not allow them to secede that the war was fought!" announced Carl triumphantly.

"Precisely! You cannot allow part of a country to rise up and walk out any more than you can let some of the wheels of a watch announce they are not going to turn any more," laughed his uncle. "It requires every part to make the watch go; and it takes the united strength of a people to make a nation. North and South were all beloved children of one land, and Abraham Lincoln, like the father of a big family, was not going to let any of the household break away from the organization to which it belonged. It meant a struggle to do the two things necessary—free the slaves and preserve the Union; but quarrels are sometimes necessary in families. After they are over there is a more perfect understanding. So it has been with this one. Both sides paid a fearful price but as a result we now have *one nation, indivisible, with liberty and justice for all.*"

"That's the oath of allegiance!" cried Carl, Mary, and Tim in chorus, as they leaped to their feet and stood at salute.

"We say it at school every morning," continued Tim, "but I never knew before what it meant."

"You will know better now, won't you?" Captain Dillingham replied. "Every time you say those words remember the brave men of the South who really believed they had a right to establish a government of their own and protect the prosperity of their part of this great land. If you do this you will learn to honor both sides alike, each of which fought so devotedly for the cause he cherished. And now that the war is over the entire country has the South to thank for one of its greatest sources of wealth—cotton. The South raises it; the North, with its many mills, transforms the raw product into a finished commodity. How is that for team work? Could there be better proof of how vitally each section needs the other?"

A LESSON IN THRIFT

That evening Carl resumed the cotton-raising subject by idly remarking, "I suppose since the invention of the cotton gin and the abolition of slavery most of the drudgery connected with the cotton industry has disappeared."

His uncle smiled.

"Hardly that, I am afraid, sonny," replied he. "Even under the best possible conditions the cultivation and gathering of the cotton crop entails drudgery. This cannot be helped. In the first place cotton demands steady heat to make it grow; and you know what it means to work all day in the broiling sun. Of course the negroes are to a certain degree accustomed to this; and moreover they belong to a race that finds hot weather less hard to bear than do many other persons. Nevertheless heat is heat, and say what you may, a hot sun pouring down on one's head does not make for comfort. In addition there is the monotony of the harvesting. As I told you before, this has to be done by hand—there is no escape from that; and since it must be, the dullness of the task is an unavoidable evil."

Carl mused thoughtfully for a moment.

"I don't see," observed he presently, "that after all the negroes are much better off than they were in slave days."

"Oh, yes, they are," Captain Dillingham instantly responded.

"Remember they now receive wages; their hours of work have also been shortened and regulated; and overseers have become more humane and now invent little ways of breaking the monotony and making the time pass more pleasantly."

"How?"

"Oh, there are various things that can be done to achieve this end. Sometimes fresh buttermilk or some other refreshing drink is passed down the rows; or on a cool day hot coffee is served. Any little change such as singing or whistling interrupts the sleepy effect of one continual process and shifts the mood and spirits of those toiling into another groove. This is very beneficial. All our students of industrial methods will tell you that the worst flaw of our present system is the effect monotony has on the minds of those constantly subjected to it. Performing without deviation the same mechanical act day after day deadens the brain and even, in certain cases, produces insanity. It also kills ambition and creates hopeless, indifferent persons. Therefore, made wiser by psychology we realize the importance of stirring the mind out of a fixed rut, or rather a stupidity that verges on somnambulism, and keeping it alert and active. Sheep growers, for example, try in every way to divert the minds of their shepherds lest the continual watching of a slowly moving flock paralyze their minds and get them *locoed*."

"Really?"

"Your mother will tell you that. That is why a shepherd's pipe is such a splendid thing. To pick out a tune and listen to it starts the mind out of its trance and promotes mental exercise. It does what gymnastics do for the body."

"But all our factories keep men at a single task," Carl objected.

"You mean the piece-work system? Aye, I know," nodded his uncle. "And as we grow wiser, and come to care more for our fellows, we begin to wonder whether so much specializing is as fine a notion as we at first thought it. It makes for efficiency, for without question a man who does just one thing over and over becomes expert at his particular job; but does he not in time, because of his very expertness, lapse into a machine whose hands move automatically and whose mind is idle? Such a result is fatal both to his intellect and his will.

He becomes passive until at length all initiative is destroyed. From many years slaves in the South reaped precisely this harvest of mental inertia. Now, thank heavens they are rousing out of the lethargy that has been their inheritance. It will however, take years, perhaps generations, for them to remedy the damage done, but if they don't give up, great results will surely come. Many of them have already shaken off their intellectual fetters so that not only are their bodies free but their minds are also. That is why I feel that all our citizens should do everything in their power to help them, and try to make up to them for the injustices they have suffered. It is not enough to take them out of physical slavery; we should break the chains of their mental imprisonment as well, through better education and opportunities."

"I'm afraid I never thought of slavery's lasting impact in that way," confessed Carl.

"A great many persons older than you do not," Captain Dillingham returned kindly. "But when you do think of them from that angle you cannot but honor them more highly, when they achieve positions of importance. Who can tell what their background has been or measure the mental exertion that has brought them where they are to-day? Wherever we meet them we should give them a hand up. We owe it to them because of our own greater opportunity."

The little man stopped to light his pipe.

"Now see where talking about picking cotton has led me," grumbled he whimsically. "A pretty distance I've wandered from my subject! Well, you mustn't touch me off on the topic of the colored race again. I have seen many abuses of the negroes in my day, both on shipboard and ashore, and the subject turns me hot. Just how the evils of cotton-gathering are to be avoided I do not know. We must wait, I fear, until some clever individual bobs up with a scheme that does away with hand harvesting of cotton. In the meantime the only remedy left us is to vary the work of the men and women who toil at it as much as is possible."

"I wish, Uncle Frederick, you would tell us just how the cotton is gathered," said Mary, who had joined the group.

Captain Dillingham flashed the girl one of his rare smiles.

"I don't know, my dear, just how much more there is to tell," declared he. "Of course, if you have ever picked currants or blackberries you will realize something of the constant bending and stooping that goes with the industry and will understand how hard it is on the back. Then there is the continual standing, a tiresome business at best. Besides, mechanically as the task is rated, it is not such an easy one after all, for the cotton fibers stick firmly to the inside of the pods and as a result the unskilled person who tries to detach them in a hurry will probably succeed only in extricating a bare half of what is inside. And like as not he will break the fibers he does get out so that their value will be sadly decreased. The trade has its tricks, you see. Furthermore an amateur generally has fragments of husks and leaves scattered through his cotton, all of which have to be removed and make extra work later on."

"Then cotton-gathering is not really such brainless work as it might be, is it, Uncle Frederick," Mary asserted.

"THE COTTON IS SENT TO FACTORIES TO BE GINNED."

"Oh, it requires a knack that comes through practice," conceded her uncle quickly. "As soon as the pods crack open and show white it is a sign the workers must be on hand for the picking, and early in the morning they assemble that they may have a long day to work while the sun is on the crop. For as I told you there can be no cotton-harvesting without sun to dry off the night's moisture. The moment a bag or basket is filled it is emptied into something larger and the picker starts afresh. Before evening comes and the dew falls, the day's crop is hurried under cover that it may not absorb any dampness. Here it is packed into receptacles banded with the owner's name or private mark, and made ready to be carried to the ginning factory."

"Don't the planters have their own cotton gins?" queried Carl in surprise.

"Oh no, son! That would be an unnecessary and expensive luxury. Just as corn is sent to the miller to be ground, so the cotton is sent to factories to be ginned, weighed, and baled for shipment. You see the cotton grown on any one plantation and cultivated under uniform conditions will be practically of the same ripeness and weight; it will also be, in all probability, of the same variety. This fact is important when ginning and selling it, and greatly increases its value. Such conditions, however, do not always prevail for there are districts (and also countries) where small cotton farms exist whose output is not large enough to make an entire bale. In such cases the product of several farms has to be combined and this makes a bale mixed in quality. This is true of part of the cotton that comes from India. There many of the natives, owing to lack of commercial and industrial enterprise, raise small batches of cotton. Often it takes a great many of these little lots to make up a bale."

"Do the natives of India take the seeds out of their own cotton?" asked Mary.

"Some of them do, using the primitive gins so long known in India. The Chinese also gin much of their own cotton by amateur gins. But it goes without saying that much of the cotton fiber is broken by these methods. For the more perfect the gin the less loss results. Even with our best machinery however, a certain amount of injury is done which cannot be avoided."

"Then Eli Whitney's gin isn't so perfect," ventured Carl.

"Its method is as perfect a one as we have," answered Captain Dillingham, "and up to date nothing better has been found. Those handling large quantities of cotton are almighty thankful to have anything as good, I can tell you. In India, China, and oriental countries, though, where the lots are small the people, as I say, still cling to their primitive foot gins. Here in America we have several types of gin all made on the same general principle but differing slightly as to detail. Some of these are better than others. By this I mean some are less brutal and cause a smaller degree of waste. Indeed I believe Whitney's own gin and those of its kind known as saw gins are considered to do the most damage to the fiber. This sort of gin consists of a series of circular saws set into a revolving shaft in such a way that the cotton fed into the machine is separated from its seeds in an incredibly short space of time. Afterward a whirling brush cleans the saws of the fiber clinging to them. It is an effectual system but a merciless one and is best adapted to short staple cotton which is strong and does not snarl. The best gins use only long, smooth blades to clear the cotton and it follows that these do the fiber far less injury."

"How does a ginning factory look, Uncle Frederick?" Carl inquired.

"You mean the inside? I never went through but one. I was waiting for a cargo at Norfolk once and as there happened to be a ginning plant near where I was staying I visited it. Generally speaking I suppose they are pretty much alike. The cotton is brought to them, as I said, in clearly marked, or branded bags or baskets, and is tossed from the wagons directly into hoppers. Afterward the contents of the hoppers is loaded into freight elevators and shot to one of the upper stories of the factory, there to be piled up and await its turn for ginning.

"When the time comes to gin that particular batch it is heaped into a hopper and borne to the gins below by means of traveling racks."

"How many gins are there to a factory?" questioned Mary.

"That depends on the size of the factory and the amount of work brought there to be done," was the reply. "A fair-sized factory in a busy district will have half-a-dozen gins or more; and when you know that one gin will clean from three hundred to three hundred and fifty pounds of cotton an hour you will see that it will take a pretty big supply to keep such a lot of machinery moving. There is a separate hopper for each gin and if the supply fed into it comes too fast it can be stopped and switched to other gins. Once in the clutch of the relentless knives the cotton is shredded apart and the seeds drop out and fall into a traveling basket. From this basket they are forced through a tube to an oil mill which usually stands in another part of the grounds."

"Cottonseed oil!" murmured Mary, recognizing an old friend. "We often use it to fry things. It's good on lettuce, too. But somehow I never thought that it was really made from the seeds of cotton."

"We often accept terms without thinking much about them,

don't we?" Captain Dillingham agreed. "But cottonseed oil is a genuine by-product of cotton."

"What is a by-product?" smiled Mary ingenuously.

"A by-product is something made from the leavings," put in Carl without hesitation. "Hash is a by-product of corned beef."

A laugh greeted the assertion.

"Technically speaking a by-product is something that is turned to account from what would otherwise have been waste. Every person who manufactures on a large scale tries to think what he can do with what is left after he has made the thing he started out to make. This he does for two reasons: first he wishes to turn back into money every ounce of material for which he has paid; secondly he desires to get rid of stuff which would otherwise accumulate and (if not combustible) force him into the added expense of carting it away. In other words he seeks to convert his waste into an asset instead of a liability. Therefore all big producers tax their brains to invent things that can be made from their waste, and such commodities are called by-products. Many of these things require no ingenuity for frequently they are articles much needed in other trades. Masons, for example, are only too thankful to have the hair taken from tanned leather to hold their plaster together; and those who dry and salt fish can easily turn the fish skins into glue. The by-products of great packing houses and tanneries are legion. Often such dealers will have at hand such a supply of usable stuff that they will establish other factories where their unused materials can be converted into cash. The sale of these products often increases very materially the profits of a business. Such a product is cottonseed oil. As millions more seeds mature each year than can possibly be used for planting why not turn them to account? Often there are from sixty-five to seventy-five pounds of seeds to a hundred pounds of cotton. Think how rapidly they would accumulate if something could not be done with them. During the war when we were unable to get olive oil from Italy and fats of all kinds were scarce we were thankful enough to fall back on the cottonseed oil made in our own country. At the oil mills machines are ready to clean the cotton seeds of lint, hull them, separate hull from kernel, and press the oil from the kernel itself. This oil is then bottled, labelled, and shipped for sale, making quite an independent little industry, you see. What is left of the crushed kernels is removed from the hydraulic presses and is remolded into small cakes to be used for——" he paused, glancing quizzically toward Carl and Mary.

"For what?" the boy asked.

"Guess!"

"I've not the most remote idea," Carl returned.

"Nor I!" echoed Mary.

"For cattle to eat," went on Captain Dillingham, completing his unfinished sentence.

"Even the hulls," he continued, "are, I believe, utilized in some way; and as I previously told you the lint which clings to the seeds is passed through a second sort of gin, gathered into a bundle, and afterward put through a carding engine which combs it out and prepares it so it can be made into wadding for coverlids, quilted linings, and quilted petticoats. All the gins then collect whatever material is left and this, being absolutely too poor for any other purpose, is sold as cotton waste to be used for cleaning machinery and polishing brass and nickel trimmings. Were we individuals half as thrifty as are manufacturers in salvaging the odds and ends that come our way we might save ourselves many a penny. Every year we Americans throw away enough food and wearing apparel to maintain a small army. We are, alas, a very wasteful people and are constantly becoming more so. Our ancestors used to lay aside buttons, string, papers, scraps of cloth and use them again. They made over clothing, fashioned rag rugs, conserved everything they could lay hands on. Their attics were museums where were horded every sort of object against the time when it might be needed. But do we follow their example? No, indeed! In fact, we go to the other extreme and hurry out of the house, either to a junk dealer or a rummage sale, everything we cannot find immediate use for. To a certain extent our mode of living has forced us to this course. Most of us reside in cramped city quarters where there are no spacious attics in which to garner up articles against a rainy day. Modern apartment dwellers boast neither attic nor cellar, to say nothing of a farmer's barn loft. Moreover, we all must scramble so fast to earn our daily bread that we have no time to make over the old; it is cheaper, we reason, to purchase new than to fuss with remodelling. Neither are materials what they were in the old days. Few of the fine old silks and woolens that would wear for a generation are to be had at present. Also we have more money than our forebears and this has much to do with our wholesale wastefulness. With plenty of everything at hand, why save? And the policy the individual is following on a small scale the nation is adopting on a much vaster one. We are using up our forests, our mines, all our resources with no thought of the morrow. We ought to stop and think about this before it is too late but I doubt if we ever will."

Captain Dillingham paused.

"There is such a thing," he added, "as people and nations being too prosperous for their own good. But to return to the cotton gin. The cotton, having been cleared of its seeds, is now known as lint, and this is bundled together until enough of it is collected to be properly baled for the spinning mills."

"What is *proper baling*?" inquired Carl.

"Why, the rough baling simply gathers the cotton together into a big bundle."

"Well, what's the matter with that?"

"Nothing—so far as it goes," laughed the Captain. "I should be sorry, however, to see many such bales coming aboard my ship."

"Why?"

"Well, you know what cotton is," answered Uncle Frederick. "After it has been picked to pieces in the gins it comes out a nice, white, fluffy mass that takes up no end of room. Were it to be transported in this condition a few hundred pounds of it would fill a ship or freight car and cost the owner so much that it would not be worth his while to transport it. Moreover, it would be bothersome to handle when it arrived at the spinning mills. Therefore before cotton is shipped it has to be reduced in bulk so that it will not take up so much space."

"But how can it be, Uncle Frederick? asked Mary, open-eyed.

"What do you do when you wish to make some soft material into a small parcel, my dear?"

"Oh, roll it up—squeeze it together," was the instant response.

"Well, there you have your answer!" responded Uncle Frederick. "Balers treat cotton lint in the same fashion; only, as they are not strong enough to accomplish this end with their hands, they resort to powerful machines, or compressors, to carry out the process for them. By means of enormous pressure they crush down the billowing lint until four feet of it can be reduced to a thickness of not more than seven inches."

"I wouldn't want to fall into that machine! chuckled Carl.

"There wouldn't be much left of you if you should, I can

assure you of that," Captain Dillingham said. "Cotton, however, does not raise any such protest. It is pressed and pressed and pressed, and while still in the presses iron bands are put round it to hold it so it can be compactly transported. An American bale of some five hundred pounds will usually have six or seven of these iron bands round it. Certain of these bales are merely rough ones; others are cylindrical. I believe the latter sort are more generally preferred. To make them the cotton is gradually pressed and rolled by powerful presses until a bale four feet long and about two feet through is obtained. These cylindrical bales weigh a trifle less than the others—about four hundred and twenty-six pounds—and because they have been pressed so hard they keep in place without either iron bands or cloth covers. When they arrive at the mills the cotton from them can be unrolled and much more easily fed into the machines. If they are covered it is merely to keep them clean."

"Do all bales of cotton have to weigh the same?" inquired Carl.

"You mean is there a standardized weight for all bales?"

"Yes."

"No, there is no universal standard for bales of cotton. The bales from different countries differ quite considerably. For example a Brazilian bale usually weighs only from a hundred and seventy-five to two hundred and twenty pounds; the Turkish from two hundred and fifty to three hundred and twenty-five pounds; those coming from India do better, averaging about three hundred and ninety pounds. Should you handle this imported cotton you would notice that the bales from India are very heavily banded, often as many as thirteen bands encircling them. This is partly because the long staple of this variety of cotton must not be injured by heavy pressure, and partly because they have not in India the excellent facilities for compressing lint that we have here. The Egyptian bales are the largest transported; they run as high as seven hundred pounds and have about eleven bands to hold them."

"It must be a stunt to get them aboard ship," grinned Carl.

"I've taken my turn at the job," responded the captain drily. "We swing them down into the hold by means of cranes and have now learned to land them quite neatly. Nevertheless, even though they are only bundles of cotton wool I should not fancy having one of them drop on my head," concluded he with a twinkle.

CHAPTER XI

A FAMILY CONGRESS

Meantime while the McGregors discussed cotton and the sunny southern fields in which it grew, Christmas was approaching and Baileyville, shrouded in wintry whiteness, began to feel the pulse of the coming holiday. Shop windows along the main street were gay with holly and scarlet. Every alluring object was displayed to entice purchasers and such objects as were not alluring were made to appear so by a garnish of ribbon or flashing tinsel. There were Christmas carpet sweepers, Christmas teakettles, Christmas coal hods and how surprised and embarrassed they must have been to find themselves dragged out of their modest corners and, arrayed in splendor, set forth before the public gaze. Nothing was too mundane to be transformed by the holiday's magic into a thing mystic and unreal. Even such a prosaic article as a washtub, borrowing luster from the season's witchery and in shining blue dress became a thing to covet and dream about.

Then there was the army of foolish trifles that owed their existence merely to the season's glamor and would have had no excuse for being at a time when the purchaser's head was level and his judgment sane. And in addition to all these there were the scores upon scores of gifts useful, fascinating, desirable, but beyond range of possibility at any ordinary period of the year.

Oh, it was a time to keep one's balance, the Christmas holidays! The very stones of the streets glistened golden and the crisp air breathed enchantment. If one's nerves were not frayed and on edge he jostled his neighbor with a smile and took his share of jostling in good part. Was not every man a brother; and did not a great throbbing kindliness emanate from all humanity?

It seemed so to Carl McGregor as the wonderful day of days drew near; and so also it seemed to all the wee McGregors. They were on tiptoe with excitement and could hardly be made to stand still long enough to have their neckties tied or their pinafores buttoned.

"Have you children decided yet what you want to do?" questioned their mother one morning, as she struggled to hold the wriggling Tim until his hair could be made presentable for school. "Christmas is but a week away now and we must come to some decision as to our plans. We can't have everything, you know. Shall it be a turkey and no tree? Or shall it be a tree and no turkey? And if it is a tree shall it be a big or a little one? We must vote on all these questions."

"I want ice-teem," lisped Nell.

"Mercy on us!" ejaculated Mrs. McGregor, in consternation, as this fresh avenue for outlay presented itself. "Nell is for ice cream and a tree too."

"And turkey!" went on the little one imperturbably. "Me wants turkey!"

"Ice-treem! Ice-treem!" cooed James Frederick.

The mother's face clouded. A tree, turkey, ice cream and presents were far beyond the range of the family purse.

"I'd rather have stockings and turkey," Mary declared.

"And cranberry sauce and nuts," put in Tim.

"And celery and sweet potatoes," added Carl. "A real dinner, Mother."

"Would you rather do that than have the tree?"

Silence greeted the question.

Into every mind flashed the picture of a tree towering to the ceiling and a-glitter with lights and ornaments. Even Carl, despite his fourteen years, could not entirely banish the vision. But the dinner, the dinner! After all the tree would only be a thing to look at; food could be eaten and enjoyed, and Carl was a healthy boy at an age when he was possessed of a particularly healthy appetite. Tempting as was the tree the aroma of browned turkey rose in his nostrils.

"I vote for turkey," announced he at last.

"No tree? No Christmas tree?" murmured Martin, his lip quivering.

"You have a tree at kindergarten, silly, and so does Nell," declared the elder brother quickly.

"'Tain't like having it here—our really own tree," bewailed Martin.

"Couldn't we have a simpler dinner, Mother, and manage to get a tree?" interrogated Mary. "It is fun to trim it and the little children love it so."

"Girls always like things that look pretty," piped Tim in disdain.

"And all boys care about is to eat and eat," Mary shot out with equal scorn.

Hidden away in a corner behind his newspaper Captain Dillingham chuckled. He was vastly amused by this family congress.

Meantime Mrs. McGregor, in order to avert the battle she saw rising, said, "Suppose we put it to vote. Are you ready for the question?"

"Yes!" responded her flock in chorus.

"All right. Shall it be presents and turkey, or presents and a tree?"

"I want mince pie," proclaimed Martin flatly.

"But we are not talking of pie, dear," answered his mother patiently. "It is the turkey we're voting on."

"I want turkey *and* a tree *and* presents *and* ice-teem *and* pie!" Nell asserted shamelessly.

"Stockings and turkey, Ma! Stockings and turkey!" shouted Carl.

"Listen, dears!" began their mother. "As I told you before we can't have everything. I wish we could but we just plain can't, so that ends it. Therefore we must choose what we think we will get the most pleasure out of. Now who is for turkey? Raise your hands!"

Every hand came up.

"And who is for a tree?"

Again every hand was raised.

Helplessly Mrs. McGregor sank back into her chair.

"Oh, dear," sighed she. "Don't you see we are getting nowhere? I told you only a minute ago we couldn't have both."

Uncle Frederick came out from behind his paper.

"See here, you young savages," began he, laughing good-humoredly, "listen to me! If you do not get down to business and use some sense, Christmas will be here and you will have nothing at all."

A wail ascended from Nell and Martin.

"Your mother can give you either turkey or a tree; but she can't give you both. In my opinion she is almighty good to do so much."

He saw the children flush uncomfortably. Carl dropped his eyes and Mary slipped a hand into her mother's.

"Now instead of clamoring at her like a lot of ungrateful little brutes and wanting the whole earth, why don't you show her you are grateful for what she's doing?" went on Captain Dillingham in a sharper tone.

"Oh, it's all right, Frederick," interrupted Mrs. McGregor hurriedly. "I don't want——"

The captain, however, was not to be stopped.

"Your mother is ready to give you turkey *or* a tree. How many are for turkey?"

Carl and Tim raised their hands.

"And who is for the tree?"

Instantly Mary, Martin, and Nell raised their hands.

"It is the tree, as I see it," acclaimed he.

"But it isn't fair," Tim objected. "James Frederick didn't vote."

At this everybody laughed and whatever tension there was vanished.

"Oh, James Frederick would vote for the tree," Mary said. "He is so little he couldn't eat turkey if we had it, could he, Mother?"

"I'm afraid he couldn't," smiled her mother. "He hasn't teeth enough."

"Then it is a tree! A tree!" cried Martin exultantly.

"Wait!" Captain Dillingham put up his hand. "We haven't finished with this matter yet. You've got your tree from your mother; now I can give you a turkey if you decide you want me to. But first you are to listen to what I have to say. A Christmas tree and a turkey mean a great deal for one family to have in these days when so many people are having so little. The O'Dowds, for example, are to have neither a Christmas dinner nor a tree; I happen to know that. Joey has been sick and there are doctor's bills to pay. Beside that, Mr. O'Dowd has been out of work and has no money to spend this year."

The little McGregors regarded their uncle with solemn faces.

"Oh, dear!" breathed Mary sympathetically.

Carl scowled soberly; then his face glowed with a sudden idea.

"Couldn't we——" he hesitated awkwardly.

"Oh, Uncle Frederick, if you *were* really going to buy a turkey, couldn't we give it to them?" flashed Mary, smiling toward her brother. "Would you mind giving it away to somebody else? You see, if you were going to buy it anyway——" she regarded her uncle timidly, "we could have something else for dinner, couldn't we, Mother? Perhaps corn chowder. We all like that. And maybe we could have a pudding and some nuts."

"Bully, Mary! I'm with you!" Carl rejoined.

"I'd like to do that, too," agreed Martin. "I wouldn't mind so much about the turkey if we had the tree."

"What do you say, Tim?" inquired Captain Dillingham.

"I don't see why we should give our turkey to somebody else," grumbled Tim sullenly. "We never have one all the year—never! You know we don't, Mother."

"No, dear; I'm afraid we don't," Mrs. McGregor said.

"Then why should we give ours away," went on Tim in an argumentative tone. "Don't we want turkey as much as the O'Dowds, I'd like to know?"

"Oh, Timmie!"

"Don't be such a pig, Tim," cut in Carl with brotherly direct-ness. "If we were hard up, wouldn't you like somebody to send you something for Christmas?"

Tim colored, his brother's question bringing home to him uncomfortable possibilities.

"We could have such fun doing it, Timmie," coaxed Mary. "Think how we could trim up the basket, and what a surprise it would be! Why, it would make no end of sport."

Tim's expression softened.

Instantly Mrs. McGregor, who was quick to interpret her children's moods, saw the battle was won.

"We can plan together what shall go into the basket," said she briskly. "Each of us might contribute the thing he likes best."

"The turkey shall be mine!" Uncle Frederick declared.

"I choose cranberry sauce!" Carl announced.

"Celery! Oh, could I put in celery, Mother?" Mary inquired. "The tops are so pretty and I love it so!"

Her mother nodded.

"Somebody must give the plain things so I will donate potatoes, squash, and onions," she said.

"Don't forget nuts! We must have nuts and raisins," Mary added.

"I'd like to give those," Tim whispered.

"You shall, son."

A friendly little glance passed between the boy and his mother.

"Pie! I want pie!" asserted Nell, who although too young to understand what was going on, nevertheless grasped the notion that food was the prevailing topic and plunged into the subject with enthusiasm.

"Bless your heart, dearie, you shall have pie!" laughed her mother. "I'll make a couple of apple pies and they shall be your present."

"There ought to be candy. Please let me send candy! May I?" begged Martin for whom the world held only two articles really worth while—candy and ice cream.

There was general merriment at this suggestion.

"Precious little candy would ever get to anybody else if you had the giving of it, Martie," teased Mary.

"Yes, Martin shall give the candy," Mrs. McGregor consented.

"We'll paste his mouth up before he goes to buy it," Carl drawled.

"Don't you s'pose I could keep from eating it if once I set out to?" scowled Martin defiantly.

"No, I don't!"

"Well, I could, so now!" The boy drew himself up proudly.

"James Frederick ought to send something, Mother," reminded the care-taking Mary. "We don't want him left out."

"Oh, we mustn't leave out the baby!" agreed Captain Dillingham. "He and I will get together and talk the matter over. There are still several things needed."

"Oh, it will be splendid!" cried Mary, clapping her hands. "Do get a real big turkey, won't you, Uncle Frederick? And we'll trim it up with a necklace of cranberries the way they do in the market."

"Huh! There you go again," sniffed Tim. "All girls seem to think of is necklaces and bows of ribbon."

Mary smiled brightly.

"What's the harm in making it pretty if you can just as well?" asked she. "I do love pretty things. Why, I believe I could eat stewed whale if it was on a pretty dish."

"I couldn't; I'd hate whale," responded the stolid Timothy.

"Oh, I didn't mean I'd really eat whale, silly," explained Mary.

"Then what did you say you would for?"

"Mary was just imagining, dear," put in Mrs. McGregor, coming to the rescue.

"She is always imagining," glowered Tim. "Only the other day she was trying to make me imagine my salt fish was chicken."

"I'll bet she didn't succeed," taunted Carl.

"Not on your life she didn't!" was the instant answer. "I know salt fish when I see it."

"No matter, dear," soothed Mrs. McGregor, affectionately touching her daughter's arm. "If in her imagining Mary can convert salt fish into chicken it is an asset that will stand her in good stead all through life. And if you, Tim, prefer to keep your salt fish just salt fish, why you have a perfect right to do so. I will say, however, that the person who has the power to make believe has an invaluable gift. Many's the time I've made believe and it has helped me over more than one hard spot. We all have to masquerade to a greater or less degree. It is simply meeting life with imagination and seeing in the humdrum something that associates it with finer and more beautiful things." For a moment she was silent; then she added in her quick, business-like accents, "And now to this dinner! There must be a basket to hold it, of course."

"A big market basket, Mother, lined with red paper. Do line it with red," pleaded Mary.

"It shall be lined with red, little lady! And trimmed with holly, too!" replied Uncle Frederick. "I will undertake to furnish both decorations along with the turkey."

"Why not put in Santa Claus napkins? I saw some paper ones the other day and they were tremendously festive," suggested Mrs. McGregor.

"I think the best plan is for us all to go together and buy the dinner," the Captain suddenly announced.

Shouts of approval greeted the plan.

"But the baby!" demurred his sister.

"We can wheel James Frederick in the carriage and take turns staying outside the shops with him," said Carl.

"And if we have the carriage we can bring home our stuff in it," put in Tim.

"Poor baby! How would you like to have a big ten-pound turkey piled on top of you?" questioned Mary indignantly.

"Oh, James Frederick won't mind," Tim responded comfortably. "And anyhow, he's got to do his bit toward making other people happy. As far as I can see he isn't denying himself anything, for he couldn't eat a turkey if it was set right under his nose. So it's his part to tote home the parcels in his flivver; he seems to be the only member of the family that has one."

Thus it was agreed and on the day before Christmas it would have done one good to witness the cavalcade of McGregors issuing forth on their altruistic pilgrimage. First went Mary, leading Nell by the hand; then Carl with Martin's mitten firmly clutched in his. Next came Mrs. McGregor with Tim, and bringing up at the rear was Uncle Frederick wheeling his namesake, the baby. What a tour it was! Certainly there never had been such a turkey as the one the reckless captain bought—a turkey so plump of breast, so white of skin, so golden of claw! Why, it was a king of birds! And then the shining coral of the cranberries, the satin gleam of the onions, the warm brown of the potatoes! As for the celery—its delicate green and faint canary tips were as good as a bouquet of flowers. Just to view its crispness was to make the mouth water. And the nuts, raisins, candy, oranges! Once in their vicinity Captain Dillingham cast aside all caution and wildly purchased one dainty after another. He seemed to have gone quite mad and it was not until his sister very positively informed him that not another bundle could be carried that he consented to be dragged away from the counters of sweet-meats.

Then staggering beneath their load of whity-brown parcels, the family hastened out to the baby carriage where Mary stood guarding James Frederick.

"Put the turkey down near his feet," cried she excitedly, as she lifted the baby in order to make more room. "The other things can be packed in round him."

"But he'll be stifled!" objected Mrs. McGregor.

"Oh, no, he won't, Ma!" contradicted Tim. "He'll probably be uncomfortable. Christmas comes but once a year, though, so he ought to be able to survive being cramped."

"Oh, James Frederick is perfectly used to having his coupé turned into an express wagon, Mother," Carl explained. "Don't worry about him. Often he rides home from down-town buried a foot deep in bundles. All that fusses me is whether the carriage will stand the strain. If it should part in the middle and the front wheels go off on an independent route it would be—"

"Both inconvenient and embarrassing," concluded Captain Dillingham with a laugh.

Fortunately, however, James Frederick's chariot was staunchly constructed and reached Mulberry Court without mishap, its precious contents—including the patient owner of the vehicle—being borne triumphantly aloft to the McGregor flat. Once upstairs the basket, scarlet paper, and holly were produced, and Mary with deft fingers went to work to fashion a receptacle worthy of the bounties with which the O'Dowds were to be surprised. At last into this garish hamper were packed the viands and afterward a card bearing holiday greetings was tied to the handle with a flaring red bow.

"Now the worst task is to come," declared Mrs. McGregor, "and that is to land the present at Julie's door without being caught. They are proud people, the O'Dowds, and I wouldn't for worlds have them know from whom the dinner comes. Timmie is not strong enough to take it and Carl is too clumsy. Should he start to run away, like as not he would stumble and bring all Mulberry Court to see what the racket was."

"Why can't I carry it?" inquired Captain Dillingham.

"You! One sight of your gold buttons would be enough, Frederick. Besides, you're none too agile in making a getaway."

"I fancy some boy could be found to leave it if I paid him," suggested the captain.

"The very thing! There's a score of 'em on the street. Fetch in the fastest runner you see, Timmie. No matter whether you know him or not. In fact, get one you don't know. 'Twill be all the better."

Away sped Tim only to return an instant later with a grimy, Italian youngster at his heels.

Captain Dillingham explained the errand.

At the sight of the gleaming quarter of a dollar the Italian grinned. He would leave a bomb or a live ox at anybody's door for a quarter, affirmed he with an ingratiating smile.

Therefore the precious basket was entrusted to him and to judge by the scampering that followed its thud before the O'Dowds' door he was quite as fleet of foot as Tim had asserted.

"Wouldn't you like to see their faces when they find it?" whispered Carl who, with Mary, was hanging over the banister, straining his ears for every sound.

There was not, however, much to hear.

After the furious knock somebody ventured into the hall. Then Julie's voice, high-pitched with excitement and consternation, exclaimed, "Mercy on us!" With that she dragged the basket into her abode and banged the door.

It was a brief drama but one entirely satisfying to the McGregors. Over and over again did Carl and Mary enact the scene to the intense delight of the family.

"Now mind, should Mrs. O'Dowd come up here with questions, you are to be careful what you say," cautioned their mother.

"But that isn't our basket, Mother," Carl said.
"This is much bigger."

"There's to be no hinting, winking, or smirking. Should Julie say anything, leave it to your uncle or me to answer. All the fun would be spoiled if you gave the secret away."

"Oh, yes," agreed Carl. "The sport is to keep folks guessing."

But no sooner were the words out of his mouth is than there was a rapping at the hall door.

"Oh, Ma! I'll bet that is Mrs. O'Dowd now!" gasped Mary.

"It can't be! She'd not track us down so quick as this," replied Mrs. McGregor, flustered and half rising.

"Most likely it's the Christmas tree, Mother," Tim suggested. "They promised to send it early this afternoon."

Again came the knock.

"I'm half afraid to open the door lest it be Julie," faltered Mrs. McGregor. "Be still a minute, all of you, till I think what I'll say to her."

But when, amid a tense hush, the door was finally opened, neither Julie O'Dowd nor the watched-for Christmas tree was on the threshold. Instead they saw a holly-decked basket so exactly a replica of the one they had given away that a cry of disappointment greeted it.

"She's sent it back!" cried Mary.

"She was offended and wouldn't take it!" murmured Mrs. McGregor. "I feared as much."

"But that isn't our basket, Mother," Carl said. "This is much bigger. Besides, we had no apples or candy bags in the one we sent."

Critically studying the gift, the family clustered around.

"It isn't our basket, Mother," Mary presently asserted. "See, this one is red."

"There must be some mistake, then," Mrs. McGregor declared. "They've left it at the wrong place."

"But our name is on it!" cried Tim.

"Where? Where?" What a bumping of heads there was as everybody bent to read the card.

"Yes, our name is on it plain as day!" replied Mrs. McGregor with a puzzled expression. Then, inspired by a solution of the mystery, she wheeled round on her brother.

"How much do you know about this, Frederick?"

"Not a thing, Nellie—I give you my word! Dearly as I should have liked to send you such a gift, my purse wasn't quite good for it," flushed the captain.

"And what wonder, with all you've spent this day," returned his sister quickly. "Then we'll count you out. But where could it have come from?"

"We don't need to leave it in the hall until we find out, do we, Mother?" Mary ventured mischievously.

"No, I suppose we don't," was the retort. "Timmie, you and Carl drag it indoors. Don't try to lift it, for you'll only be straining yourselves and maybe drop it. Let's get it into the kitchen. There may be some clue when we have a better light."

But examine it as they would, no hint as to the mysterious sender could be found.

"I guess he believes with Carl that the sport of giving a present is to keep the other person guessing," Tim remarked wickedly.

A general laugh at Carl's expense greeted the observation.

"Hush!" cautioned Mrs. McGregor. "There's somebody in the hall."

"He won't get away this time," Carl cried, springing up and throwing open the door.

"Good heavens, man! You nearly knocked me down!" cried Hal Harling, amazed by the suddenness of his welcome. "What's the matter with you? Trying to trap a burglar?" Then, glancing at the object about which the household were clustering, he added, "Jove! Have you got one, too?"

"What do you mean?"

"Why, just now somebody left a basket exactly like this at our flat. I thought maybe you folks had something to do with it and came straight over here to see. But you seem to be favored by a similar gift. They are alike as two peas. Who sent them?"

"That is precisely what we want to know," Carl replied.

"You've no idea?"

"Not the most remote."

"Hasn't Captain Dillingham?"

"I'm not guilty, if that is what you mean," the sea captain answered.

"Straight goods?" Hal insisted.

"Hang, die, and choke to death!" laughed the little old man.

"But—but—somebody sent the thing!" blustered Hal. "Why, there is everything on earth in it. Food enough to last a week. And ours has a shawl for my mother and some felt slippers for my grandfather in the bottom. And there are gloves for Louise and me. It came from somebody who knew all about us. It was no haphazard present."

"Can you beat it!" murmured Carl. "Whoever do you suppose——"

"I can't suppose. We thought it was you," announced Hal. "There's a knock at the door. Shall I go?"

Leaping forward he turned the knob, and in came Mrs. O'Dowd.

"I've had the most wonderful basket sent me that ever——" began she; then her eye fell upon the hamper in the center of the floor. "Glory be to goodness!" she ejaculated. "Wherever did you get that?"

"We don't know," Carl answered.

"And we've one just like it and can't find out who sent us ours," put in Hal Harling.

"Well, I thought for sure as you were the folks that sent me mine," declared Julie. "But if they are being scattered broadcast and you are getting one yourselves I reckon it is safe to say you don't know much about where mine came from. Well, all I can say is may the sender of them have a blessed Christmas. Owing to O'Dowd being out of work, we were to have a pretty slim celebration this year. The children were like to get nothing at all. And then just when I was trying to comfort myself with thinking how glad I should be that Joey was well, and that we all had our health even if we did lack a turkey and the fixings, along comes this windfall. Why, it is as if the heavens opened and dropped it straight down at our door. It does you good to know there are kind hearts in the world, doesn't it?"

One and all the McGregors smiled. If they wanted thanks for the self-denial they had practised they certainly had them in the gratitude that beamed from Julie's face.

"Well, it will be a royal Christmas for all of us, won't it?" went on the little woman, bustling out. "I must hurry back downstairs. The children are that crazy they are like to eat the turkey raw, claws, neck and feathers!"

"I'll come with you, Mrs. O'Dowd," said Hal. "Good-by, and a Merry Christmas, everybody."

"I'm mighty glad we sent that dinner to the O'Dowd's!" commented Carl soberly, when the door was shut and the McGregors were alone. "I'd be glad we did it even if we had no dinner of our own," he added, his eyes alight with a grave happiness.

"And I, too," whispered Tim.

CHAPTER XII

A CLUE

The next morning, fluttering excitedly round a Christmas tree spangled with tinsel and aglow with lights, the McGregors received their presents; and not they alone, for Julie O'Dowd, with her five youngsters, swelled the party, together with the Murphys and the Sullivans from the floors below. There was popcorn for everybody and satiny striped candy, and from the mysterious basket an orange for each guest was produced.

"When we have so much ourselves it would be wrong to keep it all," Mrs. McGregor had asserted; and her household fully agreed with her. Therefore the neighbors were summoned in to share in the festivity.

And after the visitors had trailed down the long stairway, shouting back their pleasure and gratitude, the wonderful dinner the hamper contained was prepared, and what a delightful ceremonial that was! Did ever any such tantalizing aroma drift upon the air as ascended from the browning turkey? Or did ever potatoes so fill their jackets to bursting? As for the celery—it was like ivory; and the cranberry jelly as transparent and glowing as a huge ruby. And, oh, the browning crust of the mince pies! So many hungry little McGregors swarmed round the stove it was a marvel some of them were not burned to death on hot stove covers or the oven door. One could scarcely baste the turkey without falling over two or three of them.

However, nobody was scalded or blistered and when at length the great bronzed bird was borne from the oven a procession of exultant children followed in the wake of the huge platter, every one of them shouting for the wishbone or a drumstick.

"Was the creature a centipede he would hardly have drumsticks to satisfy you!" laughed their mother. "Who ever saw such a lot of cannibals! Was anybody to hear your hubbub they'd think you had never had a mouthful to eat in all your lives. I don't believe your uncle ever saw worse heathen in the South Sea Islands."

Nevertheless, in spite of her caustic comment, it was plain that the mother was enjoying her children's pleasure and that Uncle Frederick was enjoying it too.

"Well," went on Mrs. McGregor, "if you do not get filled up to-day it will be your own fault. I shall put no check on anybody. You may eat all you'll hold."

Profiting by this spacious permission the McGregors fell to and what a feast they had! Never had they dreamed of such a meal. Even Carl and Martin, whose capacity appeared to be limitless, were at length forced to confess that for once in their lives they had had enough; as for Tim he sank back in his chair almost in tears because he could not find room for another mouthful.

"I couldn't squeeze down a single 'nother thing if I was paid for it," wailed he. "And I did so want a second helping of pudding! Why didn't you stop me, Ma, when I started out on that giant sweet potato?"

His mother shrugged her shoulders.

"You must learn to make your own choices," said she. "Perhaps 'twill teach you next time not to covet all you see. And now, before we begin to clear up, I want to make sure you are all content. There must be no regrets. I don't want to hear to-morrow that you wish you had had so-and-so. So think well before the food is whisked into the pantry. Has everybody had enough?"

A chorus of muffled groans arose.

"What do you think we are, Ma?" Tim managed to murmur.

"Indeed I don't know," was the grim retort. "I've often wondered. So you think you couldn't eat a morsel more?"

"*Think!* We know we couldn't," gasped Carl.

"Then sit still a second, all of you, till I take a good look at you!" commanded their mother. "That I should live to see the day when I would dish up a meal without some amongst you yammering for another helping! I'm almost tempted to take an affidavit with your signatures in black and white and preserve it in the family Bible."

With arms akimbo she viewed her grinning flock.

"Well, since you're beyond urging, we may as well turn to the dishes—that is, if anybody can stagger up and help."

Reaching over she began to remove the food from the table.

Mary sprang to aid her.

"Let me carry the things into the pantry," Tim said. "Maybe if I walk round some it will shake down what I've eaten."

"Are you laying to eat another course?" derided Carl.

"Aw, quit it!" growled Tim. "I'll bet I haven't made way with any more than you have. Here, fork over that pie! I'll put it in the closet."

"Can we trust you with it?" called Captain Dillingham.

Tim put up his hand.

"Say, I wouldn't touch that pie if you were to go down on

your knees and beg me to," Tim declared. "Millions wouldn't hire me!"

"Give it to him, Carl; he sounds perfectly safe," asserted the lad's mother. "And put those apples and figs away, too, dear, if you are going into the pantry. Mary, you and Carl pile the dishes. What an army of them there are! I believe we have out every plate we own. Martin, do take the babies into the next room where they will be out from under foot. And watch that Nell doesn't eat the candles off the tree. She's always thinking they are candy, the witch!"

"You must let me help," urged Uncle Frederick, rolling up his sleeves.

"Oh, you must not work to-day, Frederick," his sister protested. "It is a holiday and you are on shore leave. Besides, it never seems right to me to see the captain of a ship working."

"Oh, the captain of a ship knows the galley quite as well as the bridge," responded Uncle Frederick. Seizing a towel he stationed himself beside Mary who was elbow deep in the dishpan. "All hands to the pumps!" cried he sharply.

It was a ringing command and instantly Tim and Carl leaped forward to obey it.

What a dish-wiping team the three made!

Mary could scarcely wash fast enough to keep up with them.

In the meantime Mrs. McGregor was here, there, and everywhere, putting to rights the disordered house; and so effectual was her touch that by the time the last plate was on the shelf tranquillity reigned and except for lurking candy bags and stray bits of red ribbon it almost seemed as if there had never been such an event as a Christmas party.

"Now why can't we all go over to the Harlings, Ma?" Carl

inquired. "They will be through their dinner by this time. Hal asked if we couldn't come."

"But not all of us!" objected Mrs. McGregor. "Why, we're a caravan!"

"Nobody minds caravans on Christmas," pleaded Carl. "Grandfather Harling would love to see the children. We haven't had them there for ever so long."

"I suppose we might go. It isn't very far," his mother meditated.

"Oh, do let's!" Tim put in. "I'll wheel James Frederick."

"You? You couldn't wheel anything, so full are you of turkey and plum pudding! If you get there yourself you will be doing well," was the curt retort. "However, if you all want to go, I'll not hinder you. Scurry and get your caps, coats, and mittens."

Off flew the youngsters in every direction; off, too, flew Mrs. McGregor with Nell and Martin at her heels and the baby in her arms.

Owing to excitement and the general holiday confusion it was some time before there were two rubbers, two mittens, a cap, coat, and muffler for everybody; on the very brink of departure a full equipment for Martin could not be found and to his unbounded delight he was compelled to set forth in one arctic and one rubber boot—a novel combination that greatly heightened his pleasure in the trip and made him the envy of all his younger brothers and sisters. Whether his satisfaction would have outlived a long journey is uncertain for the rubber boot proved to be not only too large but treacherously leaky. Notwithstanding the fact, however, he was a sufficiently good sport to make the best of his unfortunate bargain and clatter up the long, dim flights that led to the Harlings' suite with as much spirit as the rest.

And oh, such a welcome as the family received when they did arrive!

It would have warmed the heart to see the little ones rush to Grandfather Harling, clinging round him like a swarm of bees and clamoring for a story. And a story they got—and not only one but two, three, for Grandfather was a rare story-teller and a great lover of children. Meantime the elders gossiped together, their chief topic of speculation being the sender of the wonderful Christmas dinners.

"If you hadn't got one, Carl, I should almost be tempted to think old Corcoran had sent ours to ease his conscience," Hal announced. "But of course he wouldn't have been stretching his philanthropy so far as Mulberry Court, I'm afraid."

"Oh, I'm sure the dinner couldn't have come from Mr. Corcoran," put in Louise quickly. "It wouldn't be a bit like him to tie the nuts up with fancy ribbon, and tuck in the presents. No, somebody sent that dinner who really cared, and took pains to have it pretty and tempting. Mr. Corcoran might order us a dinner at the market but he never would have packed the basket himself as—as—Mr. X did."

"Well, all I can say is that Mr. X, whoever he is, is a corker; and may he live long and prosper!" Hal declared.

"He will prosper," murmured Mrs. Harling in her soft voice. "Such a man cannot help it."

"I do wish, though, we knew who he is, don't you?" Mary asked. "I'd just like to thank him."

"I fancy Mr. X is not the sort that covets thanks," her mother replied. "Some people take their pleasure in doing a kind deed. I imagine Louise's Mr. X is one of that sort."

So they talked on, until suddenly glancing out of the window, Mrs. McGregor exclaimed in consternation, "Why, it is snowing!"

Sure enough! A thick smother of flakes whirled down into the deserted streets and cutting short Grandfather Harling's story, the visitors bundled themselves into their wraps.

"I hope the children won't take cold," said Mrs. Harling anxiously.

"Take cold? Mercy, no! They are tough as nuts, every soul of them," answered their mother. "Having no automobiles they gain it in their health. Poverty has its blessings—I'll say that! Now, Carl, you hold onto Nell and don't let her down on all fours; she is such a fat little blunderbuss! And Mary, keep Martin in the path if you can, or he will lose that huge rubber boot. Uncle Frederick is going to wheel the baby. And remember, Tim, there are to be no snowballs or snow down anybody's neck. You will have plenty of time for that sort of fun to-morrow, if you call it fun. And, children, do try to go down the stairs quietly. Don't forget there are other people on earth besides yourselves. A Merry Christmas, everybody!"

"And three cheers for Mr. X!" Hal added boyishly.

"Hal Harling, don't you dare set this brood of mine cheering in the hallway! They'll raise the roof," ejaculated Mrs. McGregor, putting up a warning finger. "Not but what I'd gladly cheer the person who sent those dinners; but we mustn't do it here."

"Well, it was a jim-dandy dinner, anyway," chuckled Hal. "We'll be eating that turkey for days. It was big as an ostrich!"

"Maybe you drew an ostrich by mistake," grinned Carl. "Who knows?"

Oh, it would have taken hearts less merry than these to be dampened by the storm! Home plodded the McGregors, shouting gaily amid the piling drifts.

"My, it is going to be a real blizzard!" Mrs. McGregor predicted. "Every tree and bush is laden already."

"The little shrubs in the park look like cotton bushes," replied Uncle Frederick over his shoulder. "Look, youngsters! You were asking about cotton when it is ripe. That is much the way it looks." He motioned toward the vista of bending foliage.

"How pretty it is!" said Mary.

"And in reality cotton is prettier by far, for there is always the blue of the sky, the gold of the sunshine, and the green of the country. It is as if one had a snowstorm in summer."

There was little opportunity for further talk for the trodden snow narrowed into a ribbon and the walkers were obliged to thread the drifts single file. At last, however, Mulberry Court came into view and with a stamping of feet and a brushing of caps and coats the family were within its welcoming portals. Then James Frederick was dug out of his carriage, shaken, and borne crowing and rosy up the stairs.

The flat proved to be warm and comfortable and while Mary lighted the lamps her mother poked up the fire and sprinkled on more coal.

"Now let's sit down everybody and have a nice, jolly evening," said she when the outer garments were all stowed away. "Come, Carl, draw up the rocker for Uncle Frederick. And, Timmie, there's room for you here beside me. What's the matter, laddie?"

For answer Tim glanced at the steely blue hands of the clock now pointing to six.

"Aren't we going to have any supper?" questioned he in an aggrieved tone.

"Supper!" exploded his mother. "Surely you are not looking for anything more to eat to-day. You yourself declared only a little while ago that you couldn't eat another morsel."

"It wasn't a little while ago; it was hours," Tim affirmed. "We've been to walk since then and I'm hungry."

"Hungry! Did you ever hear the likes! Hungry! And the bairn swallowing down turkey until I expected every second he would have apoplexy!"

"I'm hungry, too," rejoined Carl with shame-faced candor.

"So am I!" piped Martin.

"Well, I never saw your match!" cried their mother, holding up her hands. "One would think you were cobras, anacondas, or something else out of the zoo. Still, I don't see as I can let you starve. If you're hungry there's the pantry with its shelves groaning aloud with food. Run in and help yourselves."

Her family needed no second bidding. Above everything else they loved a meal where all superfluous accessories such as knives, forks, and napkins were done away with, and where there was no one at one's elbow to caution or demand the time-worn "pleases" and "thank you's." To forage in the pantry unrestrained was like being let loose in the vales of Arcadia. One after another they emerged, bearing in their hands the spoils most attracting their fancy.

"You're not going to devour that whole cross section of squash pie, are you, Tim?" asked Mary, aghast.

"Sure I am," retorted the unabashed Timothy. "That is, unless you want part of it."

"Of course I don't. But I should think you'd die!"

"I don't expect to die," returned her imperturbable brother. "And if I do I'll at least have had one everlasting good feed."

"Tim!" expostulated his horrified mother.

"Well, I will have," repeated the boy. "And anyhow, I don't believe I've eaten so much more than other folks. I notice you don't mention little Carlie here. He's worried down some food to-day, and like as not Hal Harling has, too. What's more, I'll bet a hat Hal won't go supperless to bed."

At that moment a rap came at the door and Mary sprang forward to admit the very young gentleman in question.

"You see, I'm returning your call on schedule time," grinned he, shaking the snow from his outer garments. "I can't stay but a moment; but I had to come and tell you what's happened. What do you think of that?" Diving into his pocket he held forth a handsome watch and chain.

"Who've you been robbing?" drawled Carl.

"I don't wonder you say so, kid. Can you beat it? Did you ever see such a beauty?"

"But—but—Hal, where on earth did you get a thing like that?"

"Well may you ask, kid! Think of me hitched to a gold watch! Oh, it's mine all right. Have a look inside the back cover. There's my name, you see, in perfectly good English."

"Where *did* you get it, Hal?" demanded Mrs. McGregor, as the gift traveled from one admiring hand to another.

"You'd never guess, any of you. It came from my worst enemy." The big fellow threw back his head and laughed a ringing laugh.

"But that tells us nothing. You have a million enemies," blurted out Carl.

"It certainly is from our friends we learn the truth," Hal replied with cheerfulness. "You're not a flatterer, are you, Carlie?"

"But I can't imagine who should present you with a gold watch," Carl mused, ignoring the comment.

"Oh, you're not half bright to-day. What's the matter with you?" hectored Hal, who was enjoying the sensation he had created.

"He's eaten too much turkey," Tim piped.

"I guess that's it," agreed young Harling. "Come, gather your wits together. Louise guessed the conundrum. You ought to be as smart as she is."

Vaguely Carl studied his friend's face.

"Of course it couldn't be from Corcoran," ventured he, as if thinking aimlessly.

"And why not?"

"Why, because—why Corcoran wouldn't—why should Corcoran give you a present like that?"

"The very words I said myself!"

"Do you mean to say it *was* Corcoran?"

"Well, it wasn't from Corcoran himself. But he had the buying of it. The watch came from the Corcoran kid and Midget, the dog."

"Oh!" Carl gasped, a wave of understanding flooding his face. "It was because of what you did that day. I'd almost forgotten."

"So had I. Corcoran thanked me up at the works some time afterward; you remember I told you about it. Well, I thought that was the end of the matter," Hal explained. "But evidently the Corcorans thought they wouldn't leave it there. So—" with a flourish he held up the gift.

"Oh, Hal, I think that was splendid of them," Mrs. McGregor declared. "You deserve it, too. Carl said you might have been killed that day."

"Nonsense! That's Carlie's yellow journalism. He told you a great yarn, I've no doubt. You ought to be on one of the daily papers, kid."

"But you did take an awful chance, you know you did," insisted Carl stoutly.

"Oh, you have to take a chance now and then to put a little spice into life. It was no great stunt I did," Hal protested. "I just happened to do it before anybody else did, that's all."

"I guess that's your way of putting it, laddie," Mrs. McGregor said with an affectionate smile. "Well, we're certainly glad you have the watch. It will be fine and useful. Just see you do not get it smashed to bits in some of the scraps you are mixed up in."

"Do you think I am going to stand dumb as an oyster and let somebody land a blow over my vest pocket hard enough to smash that watch, Mrs. McGregor?" interrogated the giant. "Pray, where would I be while he was doing it?"

"Gentlemen with gold watches should keep out of the prize ring," put in Uncle Frederick mischievously.

"Oh, sir, one has to have a watch to call time on the other feller," Hal retorted.

"Put it on and let's see how you look, Hal," Tim begged.

"Yes, do!" echoed Mary.

"All right, I'll dress up in it since you say the word," answered Hal, with an impish grimace. "You may as well see me in it and get used to the sight; then you won't be taking me for an alderman when you meet me on the street."

He slipped the chain through his buttonhole and the watch into his pocket.

"Don't I look for all the world like the Lord Mayor of London or one of the Common Council?"

"You look like an old sport," Carl asserted, giving his chum a blow on the chest.

Harling accepted the knock much as a kitten might have accepted a caress.

"Just for that I've half a mind not to tell you the rest of what I came for," grinned he. "I've something else to say that will set your hair on end. But you're that rude that you don't deserve to be told it."

"Oh, what is it, Hal?" Mary cried.

"Another secret!" Tim ejaculated.

"It isn't exactly a secret," Hal said. "It's a clue."

"A clue! To what, for pity's sake?" Carl murmured.

"You are thick, to-night—no mistake!" laughed Hal. "Why, what have we been arguing over all day—twisting and turning this way and that? What have we been speculating over until our brains are weak? Tell me that?"

"You haven't a clue about the Christmas baskets!" gasped Mrs. McGregor.

"I've a theory," nodded Hal, with tantalizing solemnity.

"Tell us! Tell us!" cried a chorus of voices.

"It's only a theory, remember, and it doesn't hitch up in every detail," went on Hal, quite serious now. "But it is worth considering."

"Tell us!"

"Well, it isn't much of a story, so don't get your hopes up. But the fact is that when we emptied our basket I turned it upside down——"

"Because you were still hungry!" cut in Carl.

"Exactly! How well you read me. Yes, being still famished, I thought I'd see if some last morsel of food did not lurk under the papers. So I emptied out everything and what should I find scrawled in pencil across the bottom of the basket but the word 'Coulter.'"

"*Coulter!*' shouted the McGregors in disappointed accents.

"What has that to do with it?" Carl demanded.

"Why"—Hal looked crestfallen—"why, Mr. Coulter of Davis and Coulter is one of my bosses, isn't he?"

"Y-e-s, I suppose he is. But he isn't mine. The two baskets were exactly alike and must have come from the same person; and certainly Mr. Coulter wouldn't send us a basket. Oh, you'll have to guess again, Sherlock Holmes," concluded Carl with a shrug.

"Your father used to work for Mr. Coulter at the mill," Mrs. McGregor put in in a subdued voice.

"But Dad died two years ago and Mr. Coulter never has troubled to send us anything before. Why should he begin now?" Carl argued.

"Did you examine our basket?" It was Captain Dillingham who spoke.

"No, but we can. It's out in the pantry. Run and fetch it, Martin, that's a good boy. I'm willing to bet a hat, though, ours has no 'Coulter' written on it. Yours got scrawled on somehow at the market. The name doesn't mean anything. Here's Martin now. Get out your glasses, you old detective, and look and see what you can find. If you can find Coulter on our basket, I'll eat my head," Carl hazarded with confidence.

"You hear him, witnesses," Hal said, holding up an impressive finger.

Then taking the basket from Martin, he inverted it.

"Will you never acknowledge, oh, you unbeliever, that I am wiser than you?" he presently jeered. "Come! Look at the thing yourself over here under the lamp. If that word isn't 'Coulter' I'll eat both your head and mine."

"Jove! It *is* Coulter!" was all Carl could stammer.

"What did I tell you!"

"But why should Mr. Coulter send a Christmas basket to us?" speculated Carl in an awed whisper.

"I'm not telling you why. I've not got as far as that," Hal answered. "All I said was that the name, Coulter, was written on both baskets and that the natural conclusion is that Mr. Coulter was their sender."

"I don't believe it. Why, it would be ridiculous," Carl protested. "Mr. Coulter probably never so much as heard of us in all his life. Why should he? I'm sure we don't know him."

"I'm afraid your theory isn't quite sound, Hal," rejoined Mrs. McGregor. "While it is possible that for some reason of his own Mr. Coulter, for whom you work, may have sent you a Christmas basket there is not one shred of anything to link him up with us. Mr. McGregor, it is true, was in Davis and Coulter's employ many years; but he was only one of many hundred workmen and scarcely knew old Mr. Coulter by sight. Since the old gentleman has died and the son has come into the firm the last thread that bound us to the company has been snapped. Old Mr. Coulter is gone, and McGregor, with his twenty-five years of service in the mills, is forgotten. As for this young John Coulter who has taken his father's place—I've never set eyes on him."

"But why should the name be on each of the baskets?" Hal insisted, still unwilling to surrender the idea he cherished.

"Ask the market man, laddie. It's a question for him. My notion is that in the rush somebody put it there by mistake," replied Carl's mother. "The marvel isn't that Coulter was written on the baskets; the marvel is that some word in Choctaw or Egyptian wasn't on 'em. Why, if you'd seen those clerks down at the store going round as if their heads were clean off their bodies you wouldn't wonder queer things were written on the hampers we got. I'm amazed they arrived at all."

"But somebody sent them," Hal affirmed.

"I'll join you there! Somebody sent them," nodded Mrs. McGregor. "Up to that point your arguments are perfectly logical. Those baskets never came of themselves. But as for Mr. John Coulter being their giver—why, you are mad as a March hare to think it for a moment. What would he be doing with all his college education and his years of study in Europe sending the likes of us Christmas presents? He has plenty of presents to give in his own family, I guess."

"Well, maybe you're right and the name only happened," Hal conceded. "Still, it's queer, isn't it? Queer that the name should be Coulter, I mean."

"It's a coincidence for you because you chance to work for him; but to us it means nothing."

"Yes, I can see that now," Hal agreed. "Then I guess there is nothing left before going home but to see Carlie carry out his little wager."

"My wager?" Carl repeated.

"You were going to eat your head if the name of Coulter was on the bottom of this basket, remember."

"Oh!" Carl grinned a sickly grin.

"Going to default?"

"No, not default—merely postpone the ceremony," Carl declared.

"Oh, you old crawler! Well, if you are going to put off the show I must be getting home or Mother will think I have been waylaid and my watch stolen. So long, everybody, and pleasant dreams." Then thrusting his face back into the room through the narrowing crack of the door, he added with elfish leer, "Just the same, I still think that Coulter had something to do with those baskets."

Before a protest could be raised the door banged and he was gone.

CHAPTER XIII

HAL REPEATS HIS VISIT

Whoever the mysterious Mr. X was he succeeded in keeping his identity a secret much better than did the donors of the O'Dowd's Christmas dinner. A secret when shared by too many becomes no secret at all and so, alas, it proved in this case. And yet no deliberate prattling divulged the story. Its betrayal was purely accidental.

On the morning following the holiday, which, by the way, chanced to be Sunday, Mrs. O'Dowd came up to borrow the McGregor's can opener. In Mulberry Court somebody was always borrowing. An inventory of each family's possessions gradually became public property, so that all the neighbors knew exactly where to turn for anything needed. In fact, the residents of the house so planned their purchases that they would not overlap what the dwelling already contained. Nobody thought, for example, of buying a washing machine since the Murphys had one; nor did any one see cause for investing in a wringer, when a perfectly good one was owned by the McGregors. Even such small things as egg beaters, double boilers, and ice picks, all had an established place of residence and were used in a community spirit. All day long from morning until night little boys and girls trailed up and down the long flights of stairs either to borrow or to return to their rightful owners articles that had been a-visiting. It almost required a card catalogue to keep track of where one's things were.

"Do you know who has the egg beater?" Mrs. McGregor would interrogate on a baking day.

And some of the children whose function it was to procure or carry hence the egg beater generally recalled its whereabouts.

"It's down to Murphys', Ma," Martin would shout. "Don't you remember that Thursday she was making custard?"

Oh, yes; Mrs. McGregor did recollect. It flashed into her mind at the time that with eggs so high the Murphys might well do without custard. Nevertheless, she had not said so. One did not venture to criticize one's neighbors—even if the gossip connected with the various borrowings did entail first-hand information concerning their affairs. For by common consent it was not Mulberry Court etiquette to borrow without stating exactly the service required of the article in question. When, for instance, you sent an emissary to ask for the O'Dowds' ironing board you said:

"Can Ma take the ironing board so she can iron out Mary's dress 'cause she's got to have her white one clean to speak a piece in at school."

Then the O'Dowds knew exactly why the ironing board was needed and just how necessary it was to have it, and not only did they promptly deliver it up, but the next time you met them they inquired how Mary got on speaking her piece and whether she was frightened or not. In this way a friendly interest was created.

To have borrowed the ironing board and not have detailed the accompanying facts would have been a heinous crime and would have exempted any person from loaning it. Under such circumstances it would have been perfectly excusable to send back word by the messenger:

"Mrs. O'Dowd is sorry but she is using the ironing board herself to-day."

But when Mary was to speak a piece, that was quite a different matter.

Mulberry Court had a pride in its tenants.

Mary McGregor certainly must not appear in a dress that had not been freshly ironed. Why, the people on the street would think Mulberry Court bereft of all sense of propriety! No, indeed. Mary McGregor must make a fitting showing if the whole house had to turn to to achieve the desired result. And if by any chance her family could not iron her dress, why somebody else must. Mulberry Court would make a proper showing no matter at what personal sacrifice.

And the same self-respecting spirit came to the fore on all great occasions. When the Sullivan's baby was christened was not Mrs. Sullivan arrayed in Mrs. McGregor's bonnet, Mrs. O'Dowd's coat, and Mrs. Murphy's skirt, that she might make a truly genteel impression? There was the dignity of Mulberry Court to be maintained.

Thus it followed that borrowing was no unusual act and therefore when on Sunday morning Mrs. O'Dowd presented herself at the McGregor's door and announced that she was going to have a chowder of canned corn for dinner and wanted the can opener, beyond a conversation as to the nourishment corn chowder contained; the brand of canned goods one bought; the price of it per can; the quantity of milk required and the price of that milk per quart, nothing further was said, unless it was, perhaps, to mention the crackers and inquire whether the O'Dowds used pilot biscuit or oysterettes. But of course the can opener was not denied and while Mary went to fetch it and Mrs. McGregor continued cutting Nell's hair Mrs. O'Dowd, with arms akimbo, reviewed the pleasures of the day before and compared Christmas dinners.

"Such a feast as we had," declared she. "Such turkey! It melted in your mouth and ran down your throat almost before you had the chance to taste it. And the sweet potatoes! You'd believe, actually, they were just dug up out of the ground! Had you sweet potatoes in your basket, Martin?"

"Sure we had!" returned the small boy, not to be outdone.

"And then the celery! It was that handsome it was fit to be set on a bonnet—I'm telling you the truth."

"Mary gave the celery," lisped Nell.

"Hush!" Martin cried. "You weren't to tell that."

"I didn't tell what I gave. Ma told me not to and I haven't," announced wee Nell proudly.

"But you're not to tell what anybody gave," Martin commanded. "I haven't told a thing, have I, Ma?" concluded he in triumph.

"Hush, Martin, hush!" cautioned his mother quickly. "Pay no heed to them, Mrs. O'Dowd; sure after the holiday they hardly know what they're saying."

"But—but——" Mrs. O'Dowd glanced keenly about, viewing the guilty faces and the indignant looks the older children centered on the two small culprits. She was a quick-witted woman and instantly put two and two together.

"So it was Mary sent the celery, was it?" repeated she. "And who, pray, bought the turkey?" The temptation the question presented was too great for the youthful conspirators.

"Uncle Fwedewic! Uncle Fwedewic!" cried Nell and Martin in a breath.

"He bought it wiz his very own money," Nell went on to explain before she could be stopped.

Oh, the game was all up now! Of what use was it to pretend anything after that? Martin heaved a sigh of delight. For days the secret had trembled on his tongue, making life uncomfortable and unnatural. Constitutionally it was his habit to let slip from that artless member anything that lurked at its tip and as a result he held secrets in abhorrence. Now the truth was out and he for one was glad it was. He would no longer be dreading an encounter with the O'Dowds or be under the trying necessity of acting a part.

"The candy was mine," he announced calmly. "I gave it and Uncle Frederick paid the man."

Julie ventured over the threshold.

"So it's you we have to thank for our dinner!" she exclaimed.

"You don't have us to *thank*," put in Mrs. McGregor quickly.

"But you surely wouldn't have me be taking a dinner like that and not thanking you for it," said Julie. "And neither O'Dowd nor I had an inkling! Think of our coming up here Christmas morning and all of you keeping so mum!"

"We'd have kept mum longer, if it hadn't been for Nell and Martin," Carl asserted. "I don't see why they couldn't shut up, Ma."

"A secret's no easy treasure to have in one's possession," Mrs. O'Dowd put in quickly. "And you must remember they are but mites—Nell and Martin. Indeed, in my opinion, it's a miracle they didn't blurt it out long before this. You wouldn't get a child of mine to hold his peace any such while; neither the big ones nor the little could do it. Well, well! It was a happy day you gave us and you certainly deserved the dinner you got yourselves. And you had no notion when you sent ours you were to have one of your own."

"No! When it came we thought for a moment you had sent our present back," Carl explained.

"In other words, you were going without your dinner to give it to us," commented Julie.

"We had our tree," Mary interrupted. "We didn't need both things."

"It's few would have done what you did," Julie remarked quietly. "O'Dowd and I will not be forgetting it, either."

Tears came into the eyes of the little woman and as if words failed her she wheeled about and disappeared down the dim hallway.

"At least, she was not put out by our doing it," commented Mrs. McGregor, after her neighbor had gone. "I feared some she might be. But evidently she accepted the gift just as we meant it. So that's settled! Now if we could only find out where our own dinner came from and say as much to its giver, I'd be entirely content. I've taxed my brain until my head is fair aching and still I'm no nearer having an idea where that basket of ours came from than the man in the moon."

"I guess you will just have to rate it as coming from the fairies," smiled her brother, "and let the matter rest there; that is, unless Hal Harling gets another inspiration."

"Another inspiration! Sure the inspiration he had wasn't worth much," sniffed Mrs. McGregor. "Unless he can provide a better one than that I sha'n't be listening to him."

"You may as well not be slandering him, for here he is now," Carl cried, jumping up to admit his chum whose footfall he had heard on the stairs.

"I'm not slandering him," Mrs. McGregor continued, imperturbably greeting the visitor. "In fact, what I've said about him I'd as lief say to his face. I'm telling them, laddie," said she, turning brightly to Hal, "that I have scant opinion of you as a detective."

The big fellow laughed good-humoredly.

"They are not putting me on the Scotland Yard force yet, I must own," he admitted. "But how do you know that I won't track down Mr. X yet? Give me time. No great mystery can be solved all in a minute."

"I've let you sleep on it and so far as I can see you are no better off this morning than you were last night," was the crisp retort.

"I'm not, and that's the truth," Hal returned, pulling off his coat. "I'm simply going to bury the matter the way a dog buries a bone, and then some day I'll dig it up and go to work at it again."

"I guess that's as good a scheme as any," Captain Dillingham declared. "Sometimes if you do not fuss at a riddle it solves itself. Come, sit down and talk to us while Nell gets her hair cut. It may help to keep her quiet."

The child, seated on the table and muffled to her neck in her mother's apron, brightened.

"Tell story," commanded she. "Hal tell story."

"I? Not on your life!" protested the big fellow in consternation. "I never told a story in all my days. Your uncle Frederick will tell you one."

"Uncle Frederick will do nothing of the sort," growled the captain, as he puffed contentedly at his pipe. "It's Hal who is going to tell the story. He is going to explain to us exactly what they do with the bales of cotton when they reach the mill."

"That? Oh, I can tell you that, all right, for I see it done from morning to night, year in and year out. But I don't call that a story, do you?"

"It will be a story to us, no matter what it is to you, for remember that although I have often loaded cotton and carried it hither and thither round the world I've never seen what became of it after we thumped it down on the dock."

"Haven't you? That's funny!" smiled Hal. "And yet after all I don't know as it is, either. How should you know what is done with it? I shouldn't have if I hadn't happened to spend my days at Davis and Coulter's. Well, then, as soon as we get the bales we first weigh them and make a record of each. Then they are opened up and the matted material is spread out so the coarsest of the dirt, such as leaves, sand, stems, and bits of dry pods will be loosened and fall out. To accomplish this we have opening machines of various kinds with beaters, fans, and rollers and by these methods the cotton is cleaned and pressed into a flat sheet or lap. Afterward we start in to mix the varieties in the different bales."

"What for?" questioned Carl.

"Oh, because to get good results you have to have a blend of varieties," Hal explained.

"But isn't cotton cotton?" inquired Mary.

"Not a bit it isn't," grinned young Harling. "Some cotton is far and away better than another. Often it has had better care, better weather, or better soil; or maybe it has grown more evenly and therefore has less unripe stuff mixed in with it. Or perhaps it was a finer, more highly cultivated kind in the first place. There are a score of explanations. Anyhow it is better, and because it is we do not use it all by itself. Instead we use it to grade up some that is less fine in quality. After the bales have been classified we take a little of this and a little of that until we have struck a good average. It goes without saying that we never mix two extremes, or put the best and the worst together. That wouldn't do at all. We aim to produce a mean between these two qualities. All this mixing is not, however, done by hand, as you might think to hear me talk. No, indeed! We have bale-breakers or cotton-pullers to do the work. We simply put several sheets or laps of different quality cotton one on top of another and then let the spikes of the machines tear it into fragments and mix it up."

"Oh!" Mary murmured.

"Afterward comes the scutching," went on Hal, "which is really only a continuation of the same process although the scutching machine makes the laps of cotton of more even thickness. Next we card the material to find out where we stand. It is brushed or combed out—whichever you prefer to call it, and the remaining dirt and short, unripe fibers are removed. This leaves the real thing, and the machine gathers it up and twists it into a sort of rope about an inch in diameter called a sliver."

"What a funny name!" Tim remarked.

"I suppose it is when you stop to think of it," Hal answered. "Well, anyhow, that's what a sliver is. In some mills they draw the cotton out into these long strands and double together four or eight slivers before they are carded. The carding lengthens or stretches them to the size of one and therefore you get a greater uniformity of size. Beside that, all the crossed or snarled fibers are arranged so that they lie out straight and smooth, and when this is done the material is ready for the bobbin and fly frames."

"And what, for goodness' sake, might those be?" demanded Captain Dillingham.

"I certainly am a great hero coming here and knowing so much," Hal answered with amusement. "I think you will understand them better, sir, if you forget what they're called and remember only what they do. They actually combine three processes: slubbing, intermediate, and roving, and their aim is to draw the sliver out until it is thinner, more uniform, and cleaner for spinning. Surely that is simple enough. The spinning is done on a mule or a ring frame—sometimes the one is preferred, sometimes the other. Generally speaking, the thread from one of these machines is what is used for weaving purposes. Sometimes, though, it happens that an order comes for a crackajack fine yarn of the best possible quality and then another combing or carding process follows which takes out everything shorter than fibers of a specified length. As a result about seventeen percent of waste is thrown out, as great a percentage as in all the other processes put together. Naturally it is a pretty expensive operation and it makes the yarn thus turned out high in price."

"I suppose such yarn goes only into the finest quality goods," observed Captain Dillingham.

"Exactly!" was Hal's answer.

"It all sounds simple as rolling off a log," Carl affirmed.

"If it seems so to you, just you think back over the problem Arkwright and some of the other inventors, the fruit of whose labors we are now reaping, had to solve," put in Uncle Frederick. "Even I, who am ignorant as an Egyptian mummy concerning cotton manufacture, can appreciate to some extent what they were up against. You must remember that no material is stronger than its weakest part. You have, for instance, a thin place in a string; it matters not how strong that string may be in other spots; pull it taut and it will snap. The thick places do not help make the string strong as a whole. So it is with thread. You have to draw it out until every portion of it is as strong as every other—a pretty little conundrum! It is the drawing, twisting, and doubling which makes the thread first uniform and then strong. Try working-out devices that shall do all these things—devices that shall twist and then double without untwisting, for example. You'll find it worse than a three-ringed circus."

"That's right, sir!" Hal agreed heartily. "I remember when I first went into the mills how puzzled I was at seeing the bobbins whirling in opposite directions. It seemed as if one was simply undoing what another had done. I thought they all ought to turn the same way. It was months before I got through my head what they were up to."

"I hadn't thought of the twisting and doubling part," Carl murmured.

"You decide with that thrown in maybe the answer to the puzzle isn't so easy, eh?" responded Hal with a teasing smile.

"I might have to ponder over it," Carl confessed suavely.

"Ponder! I guess you would. What's more, you'd have a good smart headache before you were through your *pondering*, I'll bet!" jeered Hal, tweaking his chum's hair.

CHAPTER XIV

SPINNING YARNS

All good things, alas, come to an end and the McGregor's Christmas holidays were no exception to this immutable law. A day arrived when Carl, Mary and Tim were obliged to return to school, and following swift on the heels of this dire occasion came a yet more lamentable one when Uncle Frederick Dillingham was forced to go back to his ship and sail for China. The latter calamity entirely overshadowed the former and was a very real blow not only to Mulberry Court, where the captain had become an object of universal pride and affection, but also to the Harling family who had come to depend on his daily visits for cheer and sunshine.

"I don't see why somebody else can't sail your ship to China, Uncle Frederick, and let you stay here," wailed Mary.

"Somebody else sail my ship!" gasped the captain, every syllable of the phrase echoing consternation. "Why, my dear child, I would no more turn the command of the *Charlotte* over to another person than you would exchange your mother for somebody else's. The *Charlotte* kind of belongs to me, don't you see? She is my—well, I reckon I can't just explain what she is. All I can say is that where she goes I go—if I am alive."

"But—but the sea is so terrible," objected the timid Mary. "So dangerous."

For answer Captain Dillingham burst into a peal of laughter.

"Dangerous? Why, lassie, there isn't a quarter a part the danger on the water there is on land. I have come nearer to being killed right here in Baileyville than ever I have while cruising in mid-ocean. Folks take their lives in their hands every time they cross a city street. Then, too, aren't there high buildings to topple over; flagpoles to snap asunder, signs to blow down; chimneys to shower their bricks on your head; not to mention the death-dealing currents that come through telegraph and telephone wires? Add to this threatening collection trees and snow-slides and slippery pavements and you have quite a list of horrors. Danger! Why, the land is nothing but maelstrom of catastrophes compared with which the serenity of the open sea, with nothing but its moon and stars overhead, is an oasis of safety. Of course there are certain things you must be on your guard against while on the water—fogs, icebergs and gales. But where can you find a spot under God's heaven entirely free from the possibilities of mishap of some sort? I'd a hundred times rather take the risks the sea holds than run my chances on land. Besides, aren't we a city, same as you? Just because we are afloat and you can boast the solid ground under your feet is it a sign we are not citizens with laws and duties, with the wireless singing its messages to us wherever we go we certainly are not cut off from the rest of the world."

For a moment he paused to catch his breath.

"No, siree!" continued he. "We folks on shipboard simply belong to a floating republic, that's all. It's our country same as this is yours, and we love it quite as much as you do."

"I never thought of the ocean that way," Mary returned with a thoughtful smile. "It's always seemed to me a big, big place without any—any streets or——"

"But we have streets, lassie," cried her uncle, instantly catching her up. "Regular avenues they are. Travel 'em and you'll meet the passing same as you would were you to drive along a boulevard. They are the ocean highways, the latitudes and longitudes found to be the best paths between given countries. In some cases the way chosen is shorter; or maybe experience has proved it to be freer from fog or icebergs. Anyhow, it has become an accepted thoroughfare and is as familiar to seafaring men as if it had been smoothed down with a steam roller and had a signpost set to mark it. Never think, child, of the ocean as a lonely, uncharted waste of water. It is a nice quiet place with as much sociability on it as a man wants. You don't, to be sure, rub elbows with your neighbors as you do ashore; but on the other hand you don't have to put up with their racket. Pleasant as it is to be on land the hum of it gets on my nerves in time, and I am always thankful to be back aboard ship."

"We'll miss you dreadfully, Frederick," his sister remarked.

"But remember I'll be putting in at various ports off and on," returned the captain, "and be mailing you letters, postals and trinkets of one sort and another. Moreover, you're all going to write to me, I hope—even Martin. For if there's any one thing a sailor man looks forward to it's the mail that awaits him in a foreign port. I must own that with all the virtues the sea possesses the landlubber has the best of us on mail service. Rural free delivery is one blessing we can't boast. No blue-coated postmen come sauntering down our watery streets to drop letters and papers into our boxes. We have to call for these ourselves same as you might have to go to a post-office here ashore if the government wasn't as thoughtful and generous as it is. Our post-offices are sometimes pretty far apart, too, and I'm driven to confess we don't always get our mail as often as we'd like.

That's one of the outs of seafaring. So when we do touch shore and go looking for letters it is disappointing not to find any. Don't forget that. After I'm gone you will get busy with your school, and your sewing, and your fun, and you will not think so often about Uncle Frederick." He put up a warning hand to stay the protest of his listeners. "You won't mean to," continued he kindly, "but you'll do it all the same. It's human nature."

This sinister prediction, however, did not prove true.

For days after Captain Dillingham said good-by to Baileyville, Mulberry Court, the Harlings and the McGregors were inconsolable.

"The house isn't the same with Uncle Frederick gone, is it, Mother?" commented Mary.

"No, it isn't. We miss him very much."

"I should say we did! Such a lot of things happen all the time that I want to tell him," Carl broke in. "Why, only this morning the teacher gave me a book to look up something and the first page I opened to had a lot about foreign trade. A month ago I wouldn't have cast my eye over it a second time but now, because of Uncle Frederick, that sort of thing interests me. So I read along down the left-hand column and what should it be about but the first spinning mills! I wished Uncle Frederick could have read it."

"You must write him about it," flashed Mary. "What did it say, Carl?"

"Oh, I don't know," her brother answered awkwardly. "I'm not sure that I can remember exactly. I wasn't learning it to recite."

"But you read it, didn't you?"

"Sure I did, Miss Schoolmarm!"

"Then you must remember some of it," Mary persisted.

"Oh, I remember scraps of it. It said at the outset that nobody really knew when people began to spin. Most likely they got the idea from pulling out fibers of cotton or wool long as they could make them with their fingers, and then twisting the stuff together into larger and longer threads. As they could do this better if they had the end fastened to something, they got the notion of using a stick or some sort of spool or spindle to wind the thread up on as they made it. They would go walking round with a mass of material under one arm and this crude spindle with the thread on it under the other. The book said that even now in certain foreign countries there were peasants who did this. It was during the reign of Henry VII that spindles and distaffs first appeared in England. Afterward people improved on the idea and made spinning wheels. The people of India had had these long before, so you see they weren't really new; but they were new to England. To judge from the book they weren't any great shakes of spinning wheels; still they were better than nothing. Later on the English got finer ones such as were used in Savoy and these not only had a spindle but a flyer and bobbin. It was most likely these Saxony wheels that started inventors trying to make something that would be better yet."

Holding the plug he was whittling for his double-runner up to the light, Carl halted.

"I think you've done pretty well, son," remarked his mother over the top of her sewing.

"I think so too," Carl returned with unaffected candor. "I had no idea when I started that I could remember so much. I guess it was because I was interested in the story and wasn't trying to learn it. When you think you're learning things, you get to saying them over and over until by and by what little sense there is in 'em seems to evaporate. At least, that's the way it is with me. If I could just read and not keep thinking that I was trying to learn I'd get on twice as well. Even this page of stuff would have *looked* different if I'd been going to learn it. You see, you never have the chance to learn what you want to at school; it's always what they pick out for you. Naturally you don't care as much about it as you would if it was what you'd chosen yourself."

Mrs. McGregor could not resist smiling in sympathy with this philosophy of education, novel as it was.

"Now what the teacher sent me to look up in that book," went on Carl, "was some old foreign treaty. Of course I read it over because she made me. But do I remember a line of it? Nix! I told her what the book said as fast as I could, so to get it off my soul before I forgot it. I don't see what she cared about it for anyway, for it didn't seem to hitch up to anything. But this spinning business hitched right up to Uncle Frederick, Hal Harling and what we've been talking about. I don't see why Miss Dewey couldn't have let me alone to learn about that."

"Probably she didn't dream you were interested in it," said Mary. "How should she, pray?"

"I know it. I suppose she didn't," answered Carl with fairness. "She certainly is no mind reader; and I didn't mention it."

"Then don't go blaming poor Miss Dewey," Mary retorted. "Besides, what kind of a school would she have if every child in it refused to learn anything but what he cared about. She would have fifty kids all going fifty different ways."

Carl sighed. Plainly the flaws of the educational system were too many for him. Nevertheless he attempted a modest defense of his theory.

"No, she wouldn't," contradicted he. "Some of 'em don't want to learn anything anyhow, and since they have to they are as well pleased to learn one thing as another. Billie Tarbox, for instance, hasn't any preferences; he just hates all highbrow stuff alike. And the Murphys and Jack Sullivan wouldn't care a hurrah what they learned. All Jack wants to do when he grows up is to run a steam roller and if he can do that he'll be perfectly satisfied."

"But he'll have to learn something before he can," observed Mrs. McGregor.

"No, he won't, Ma. Mike Finnerty who lives in his block runs one and he doesn't know a thing," Carl replied simply.

"On the contrary, I think you'll find Mr. Michael Finnerty knows much more than you give him credit for," retorted Mrs. McGregor. "He probably knows more than he himself realizes. He may not have learned about engines out of books; but if not he has learned about them from actual contact with them. All learning does not come from between book covers, sonny. Experience is a wonderful teacher. Books simply give us the same result without making us stumble along to learn everything ourselves. They are somebody else's experience done up in a little bundle and handed to us as a shorter cut. Mr. Michael Finnerty has had to take the long way round to get his education, that is all. For education is nothing but a training which enables us to live and be useful to others; and if when we're through we can't do that all the book learning in the world isn't going to be worth much to us."

"Why, Mother, I thought you were terribly keen on schools," ejaculated Mary, aghast.

"So I am, my dear. A fine mind thoroughly trained is a glorious tool; but far too often people forget that it is simply a tool. Just sharpening and polishing it and never turning it to account for other people isn't what it was made for. Learn all you can so you will be able to help the world along the better. But don't just soak up and soak up what books tell you and then store it away in your head like so much old lumber."

"But what can you do with what you read, Ma?" Carl questioned, laying down his whittling and facing his mother.

"Precisely what you have been doing this morning, for one thing," was the quiet answer. "Pass it on to somebody else who hasn't read it. Mary and I, for example, hadn't read about England and the early spinning wheels. We hadn't the time to; nor had we the book. You've managed to tell us quite a lot."

"Maybe I could tell you some more, if you wanted me to," said Carl, urged on by altruistic impulse.

"Of course we do," his mother replied.

Carl took a long breath and considered thoughtfully.

"Well, what knocked me was that at first the English government didn't want any cotton cloth made," began he.

"Why not? I should think they would have been delighted!" Mary put in.

"Oh, the English made a lot of woolen goods, and they had a hunch that cotton cloth might cut into the trade for wool and fustians. So Parliament passed a law placing a five-pound fine on any of the British who wore things made of colored calico. As the restriction also covered the use of painted, dyed or stenciled cottons it knocked out all these products for hangings, bedspreads, or coverings."

"How horrid of them!" said Mary indignantly.

"They were darned afraid of their trade being interfered with, you see," explained her brother. "I believe you could use an all blue calico and of course there was no objection to making cotton cloth into underclothes; also you were allowed to use a cloth woven of cotton and wool. But you mustn't wear any pretty figured cotton dresses. When the people heard that they kind of rose up, and when the government found out they wouldn't stand for such a law, in 1736, after amending it, they made another one letting folks wear any kind of decorated cloth they had a mind to, so long as its warp was entirely of linen yarn. This provided England with a market for her flax. But once the law was passed the delighted manufacturers began to turn out colored cloth by the bushelful, making any amount more than they could sell just because they were allowed to. This led to another difficulty—where were they going to get enough linen warp? The cottagers who worked at home with their little spinning wheels could not begin to turn out the supply that was needed, and weavers of cloth went traveling everywhere over England buying up all the linen thread people would sell and begging for more. And not only did they want linen warp but they wanted it stronger and coarser so they could weave heavier cloth. Now the spinning wheels only turned out single thread. What was to be done?"

"Well, what was to be done?" echoed Mary.

"It was trying to find an answer to all this weaving muddle that set John Kay to inventing his flying shuttle," replied Carl. "Until then it had taken two people to send the heavy shuttles with the warp on them across the looms. His new flying shuttle did the same work with only one person to operate it. You'd think that an improvement in weaving, wouldn't you; and you'd have the right, if you worked out the idea, to believe the weavers would be pleased?"

"Certainly," returned his mother.

"Well, instead of being pleased, the workmen were crazy," Carl announced.

"Why?"

"Because they were such blockheads they were afraid Kay's invention was going to put them out of their jobs. In fact, they got so soured on poor old Kay that his life was actually in danger and he had to get out of England. There's gratitude for you!" concluded the boy with a shrug.

"But later on they learned better, I suppose, and sent for him to come back," Mary suggested. "That's the way people always do."

"These people didn't," was Carl's grim retort. "Not on your tin-type! They never got Kay back again in spite of all he'd done for them. Instead, he died somewhere abroad without receiving much of anything for his invention. Wouldn't that make you hot? In the meantime, about 1738, a chap called Lewis Paul got out a double set of rollers that would draw out thread and twist it—a stunt previously done by hand. So it went. Here and there men all over England, knowing the need of better spinning devices, went to it to see what they could do. John Wyatt, who, like Paul, was a Birmingham native, tried spinning by means of rollers; and for ever so long it was a question whether it was he or Paul who should be credited with the invention of the roller and flyer machine. After twenty years I believe Paul was granted the patent. In point of fact, though, Arkwright thirty years before had tried to get a patent on spinning by rollers, and no doubt both Lewis Paul and John Wyatt got the suggestion from him. Anyhow, the idea spread like wildfire and immediately no end of people went to work fussing with rollers, flyers, and spindles. As a result, many small things were added to improve the spinning contrivances in use at the time. Then in 1764, or thereabouts, along came James Hargreaves, a Lancashire Englishman, with a machine that would spin eleven threads at once."

His listeners gave a little gasp.

"That was some stride ahead, wasn't it?" commented Carl, as proudly as if he himself had done the deed. "Yes, siree! Hargreaves's spinning jenny was a big step forward. And as usual it raised a row. When he got it all perfected five years later and went to take out a patent on it, his right to it was questioned and his life made miserable. But, anyhow, people couldn't say he built on Arkwright or Paul, for whether they liked it or not they had to admit his idea was quite new. His jenny only spun cloth rovings, however. The rovings had to be prepared first; that is, the cotton had to be carded and given its first twist. After that Hargreaves was ready for it and could lengthen, twist, and spin into yarn eleven threads of it."

"I hope the ungrateful workmen did not get after him as they did after John Kay," Mary murmured.

"They did! At least, although they did not drive him out of England they drove him out of Lancashire. So he went to Nottingham; and after arming himself with his patent he and a Mr. James built a spinning mill there, one of the first to be built in England."

"That must have made his fortune and repaid him for all his hard labor," remarked Mrs. McGregor, as she held up a violet cloud of spangled tulle and examined it critically.

"The book said he didn't make much money," Carl announced. "He wasn't as poor as John Kay and did not die in want; but he certainly never became rich."

"I suppose now that they had spinning factories England was satisfied," said Mary.

"Satisfied?" repeated Carl with scorn. "Satisfied because there was one little measly spinning factory? You bet your life people weren't satisfied! To be sure some of the hardest of the inventing was done. But don't for a minute imagine you are through with Richard Arkwright. He was still on the job."

"You told us about him before."

"Trying to get a patent on spinning by rollers? Yes, I did.

Well, he was still alive and of course when everybody was talking about spinning he couldn't help hearing the gossip even if he did happen to be a barber. In fact while he traveled round buying and selling hair for wigs he must have met no end of people and talked with them, so I guess he heard more of the news of the day than did lots of other men. Barbers always seem to be sociable chaps. He was quite a mechanic, too, in his way; machinery had always interested him."

"In spite of his making wigs and toupees for ladies and gentlemen?" laughed Mrs. McGregor mischievously.

"Sure, Ma! He had been born in Lancashire just as Hargreaves had and so he probably was particularly interested in Hargreaves. When anybody from your own part of the world does anything smart you always are all ears about it, you know. So Arkwright found out all he could by gossiping about Hargreaves's spinning jenny, and no one was quicker to see what such an invention would mean to England than he. The idea was almost like a magnet to him. He hunted up Mr. Highs, who had experimented a lot with spinning machinery, and talked with him; he also met John Kay, who at one time had helped Highs. And because he was such an intelligent listener and seemed to understand machinery so well these men babbled to him about their hobby. Having heard all they had to say Arkwright went off by himself and set quietly to work to try out on a small scale certain notions of his own. These notions had to do with spinning cotton by drawing rollers, and they worked perfectly. That was enough for him. He announced his success, got his patent, was knighted by the crown, and became rich. How's that for a yarn? Isn't it like the story of Puss-In-Boots?"

"It is certainly magical," declared Mrs. McGregor, who had dropped her work in her absorption. "I am glad, too, to know there was one inventor who prospered."

"I am afraid he was the only one—at least of those interested in spinning," replied Carl gravely.

"All the others both before and after him lost out so far as money went."

"Who did come after Arkwright?" queried Mary.

"Crompton—Samuel Crompton," was the prompt reply. "He was a little boy when Arkwright was tooting round the country trading hair and wigs. The two men may even have happened to see one another somewhere. That wouldn't be impossible, you know. Anyway, during the time that Arkwright was fighting the right to his roller patent; going into partnership with rich men who could finance his schemes; and building his chain of mills at Nottingham, Cromford, and Matlock, Crompton was growing up. As some of these mills were worked by horse power and some by water power, the name of 'water frame' clung to Arkwright's invention. Crompton, like everybody else who lived at the time, saw the rivalry between Hargreaves's jenny and Arkwright's water frame. It was of course silly that there should have been rivalry, for the two machines did quite different sorts of work. Arkwright's water frame was better for making the warp and long threads of cloth; and Hargreaves's jenny turned out better weft, or the kind of thread that went from side to side. It was only a matter of the sort of thread you needed, understand."

"Then they certainly needn't have been jealous of one another," commented Mrs. McGregor.

"Fortunately in time they found that out and realized that each loom had its advantages; to-day both are used—one for one purpose, one for another. But no matter how many enemies Arkwright had everybody, whether they liked him or not, was compelled to admit that he gave the spinning industry a tremendous boost and did more toward starting our present factory idea than did any one else. Not only was he a tireless worker, but he was quick as a flash to see what was needed. Maybe he wasn't any too scrupulous whose property he took; but at least he took the things he seized more for the public good than his own, I really believe. For instance, there was Lewis Paul's carding engine; he introduced that into Lancashire and added to it a stripping comb, or doffer, that made it about fifty percent better than it ever had been before. That is what he did to everything he touched. He swooped down on any machine he saw and then proceeded to improve it. It didn't matter to him who it belonged to. Of course you can't do that, even if you are an inventor," grinned Carl. "Naturally it got Arkwright in wrong and he was given some pretty hard names. Still he did a lot of good for all that. And, anyway, whatever he was, I take my hat off to him because he began to study writing, spelling, and arithmetic when he was fifty years old. That gets me!"

"Poor soul! He probably had no chance for an education when he was younger," remarked Mrs. McGregor.

"No, he hadn't. But picture it! Jove! If I had gone that long without books, and had been able to invent all sorts of things into the bargain, darned if I wouldn't have stuck it out," Carl said.

"But you told us Arkwright became rich and was knighted," replied Mrs. McGregor. "No doubt this resulted in his meeting educated people, gentlemen and ladies, in whose company he felt ashamed, uncomfortable, and at a disadvantage."

"I'd feel that way, wouldn't you?" nodded Mary. "I do feel so even when I am with Uncle Frederick, and my teacher, and— and you, Mother."

"Don't include me, dear," protested her mother sadly. "Alas, I know little enough. But it does help you to understand how that poor, hard-working Richard Arkwright suffered. Often, I'll wager, he was angry at himself for his lack of education even though it was not his fault. I don't wonder, snubbed as he probably was at times, that he determined he would learn something."

"His hard-earned education did not do him much good, Mother, for he died when he was sixty," said Carl.

"Well, at least he lived long enough to see his success," Mary put in brightly.

"He was luckier than Crompton," replied her brother.

"Oh, tell us about Crompton. Do you remember anything about him?" Mary inquired.

"Crompton was one of the most important of the spinning inventors," continued Carl. "But he did not set out to be an inventor any more than Arkwright did. To be sure he wasn't a barber or anything as ordinary as that. He was a musician, a person of quite another sort, you see. His family were better bred and started him out with a good education—the very thing Arkwright lacked. Crompton might easily have mixed with the class Arkwright wanted to mix with but he wasn't as good a mixer. Instead of gossiping with everybody he met, as Arkwright had done, Crompton kept by himself and lived quietly at home with his mother."

"A sensible lad!" Mrs. McGregor whispered.

"Maybe," grinned her son. "Still, it made people call Crompton unsociable. I guess, though, most geniuses are that. They always seem to be so in books; and Crompton certainly was a genius. He hadn't an ounce of brain for business but he had no end of ideas; and it was those that got him on in life. For you see, although the Cromptons were what Ma would call 'gentle people', they were not rich. They were comfortably off, though, and if the father had not died when the children were small they might have been very well off indeed. As it was, Mrs. Crompton had to help out the finances by carding, spinning, and weaving cloth at home when her other work was done. Ever so many other women did it, so it was considered an all right thing to do. Since Kay's flying shuttle had made it possible to spin more stuff the weavers, as I told you, were scouring the country for all the warp and weft they could lay hands on, so everybody who could spin thread was sure of a market. The prices offered, and the difficulties the weavers were having to get material enough, were common talk at every English cottage fireside. So of course it wasn't strange that Mrs. Crompton, along with the rest of her neighbors, heard this gossip and also heard about Hargreaves's spinning jenny. Now Samuel helped his mother to spin evenings when he wasn't playing at the village theater and she decided it would be nice to get one of these spinning jennies for him to use. So she did, and it wasn't long before he could not only use it, but could turn out weft enough for cloth to clothe the whole Crompton family."

"Then I don't see but the Cromptons were nicely taken care of," Mary announced.

"That wasn't the point, smartie!" her brother objected. "Of course they were well enough off themselves, but the village of Bolton where they lived was strong on its muslins and quilt materials and what the people wanted was to be able to spin fine muslins such as were imported into England from India and China. If such goods could be made by Orientals why should not people as clever and ingenious as the English make them?"

"Why, indeed?"

"They couldn't do it; I don't know why," answered Carl. "They just could not contrive to draw fine enough thread. Of course

Samuel Crompton had always seen the Bolton goods since he was a little boy and so knew as well as did everybody else in the town what a wonderful thing it would be if finer thread could be made. So after his mother got her spinning jenny for him he began to fuss round with it simply to find out whether he could make it any better or not. He experimented five years and at the end of that time he had made a 'muslin wheel' that was something like Arkwright's water frame and something like Hargreaves's jenny and yet wasn't like either of those things. Therefore, as a joke, it was called a 'mule.'"

"Oh, I'm awfully glad he made it!" ejaculated the sympathetic Mary. "Five years was such a long time to work. Wasn't it splendid of him!"

"Other people, I'm sorry to say, were not of your opinion," Carl replied. "As I said before, the spinners and weavers were a crazy, jealous lot. You remember how they treated Kay and Hargreaves? Well, they hadn't improved any and were still just as mad at spinning inventions and spinning inventors as they were before. Everything that did away with hand labor was, they argued, an enemy and was going to put them out of business."

"But how could they expect they were going to stop the progress of the world?" asked Mrs. McGregor.

"They didn't think it was progress; they were just that stupid," returned Carl. "And I guess even if they had thought so it would have been the same. They were determined to use nothing that reduced the number of hand workers. So they set themselves to take out their vengeance on all spinning machinery, and in order to put an end to it mobs of workers went about smashing to atoms every spinning jenny they could find that had more than twenty spindles."

"How nasty!" breathed Mary.

"How stupid!" rejoined her mother.

"Now, of course, Samuel Crompton wasn't going to have his new 'muslin wheel' smashed to bits so he did not tell anybody what he had invented. He simply took the thing to pieces and hid the parts round his workroom. Some of them he put in the ceiling, some he tucked away under the floor."

"Bully for him!" Mary cried. "It was a regular kid trick."

"I know it," agreed Carl. "He wasn't really a kid, though, because he was twenty-seven years old at the time and was married and his wife had just come to live at the big Crompton homestead. Well, after a little while, things settled down and then Samuel Crompton dragged out the parts of his hidden muslin wheel, put them together, and he and the lady he had married went to work making the finest and strongest yarn they could. Such fine thread had never before been made in all England and you better believe when it began to appear it created a stir. Everybody in Bolton went round trying to find out where it came from and after the tidings spread about that the Cromptons were the people who were producing the mysterious yarn, the town swelled with pride. How was the thread made? That was the next question!"

"And the Cromptons didn't tell, of course."

"That's where you're wrong, Mary Ann! I wish they hadn't; but they did."

"That was a pity," interrupted Mrs. McGregor.

"You'd have thought they would have been wise enough not to, wouldn't you?" Carl observed. "But I told you Samuel Crompton had no great head for business. He was trusting and decent, just the way Eli Whitney was. He had no idea people would steal his invention. So when the mill owners and factory folks came surging to his house, he not only let them see the loom but even allowed some of them to try it when they wrote out a promise or pledged their word that they would pay him for the privilege."

Mrs. McGregor shook her head.

"I'm afraid," said she, "that was all he ever heard of the money."

"Of course it was, Ma! Evidently you know more about human nature than poor Crompton did. He was utterly amazed when they wouldn't pay up. And when there were others mean enough to hide in the room over his workshop, bore holes in the floor, and spy down at the magic machine, all was lost."

"He held no patent, then?"

"He hadn't one thing to protect him. The sharks just came down on him, grabbed his idea, and walked away with it unmolested," answered Carl.

"Oh, that was pitiful—pitiful!" exclaimed Mrs. McGregor, laying aside her work.

"It was a darn shame!" echoed her son.

"And the Cromptons never got any money at all?" asked Mary.

"Not then, anyhow."

"Well, at least Mr. Crompton had the joy of doing what he set out to do—nobody could take that satisfaction away from him," mused Mrs. McGregor.

"Yes, but would that have consoled you for finding that people were so low-down?" answered Carl with scorn. "I'll bet that one fact disappointed him more than the loss of the money. It would me."

"Greed, I regret to say, sonny, is at the bottom of most of the evils of the world," retorted his mother sadly. "What finally became of the Cromptons?"

"Oh, the whole thing got on Crompton's nerves and he moved to another town where he buried himself," Carl answered. "After a while, though, he came back to Bolton because he needed money and opened a little factory there. It ran along for almost ten years, doing business on a small scale. Imagine it! Then in 1800 some Manchester manufacturers (who had probably got rich on his invention and whose consciences troubled them most likely) collected a purse for him that his mill might be enlarged. By this time as a result of various improvements Crompton's idea had expanded until one of his looms had as many as three hundred and sixty spindles, and another had two hundred and twenty."

"And years before the spinners had destroyed those that boasted more than twenty," commented Mary thoughtfully.

"I know it! Ironic, wasn't it? Poor old Crompton! He just didn't seem to have any luck," asserted Carl.

"It wasn't want of luck, my dear, so much as want of wisdom—the wit to grasp opportunity when it came," contradicted his mother.

"You mean 'there is a tide in the affairs of men', Ma, and all that?" Carl grinned. "Who says I don't know Shakespeare when I meet him? Anyhow, I guess Bill was right; he certainly was in this case. Even the money the English government later collected and presented to Crompton got dribbled away and lost in various unfortunate enterprises. Crompton got poorer and poorer, and if it hadn't been that friends took care of him he might almost have starved."

"And did his star never rise again?" inquired Mrs. McGregor.

"Never! He just died in poverty and left other people to grow rich on what he had done."

"That is the world, I am afraid," was Mrs. McGregor's observation. "Still he had given humanity a hand up and done a great service to his generation. That knowledge was better than all the fortunes he could have possessed."

"But he might so easily have had both, Ma," returned the practical Carl. "I call the help to humanity slim comfort when you've been cheated out of what should have been yours. I shouldn't even have been grateful had I been Crompton for the fine monument they set up to his memory long after he was dead. What they ought to have done was to treat him square while he was alive to enjoy it."

"See that as you go through life you do not forget your own philosophy, my son," cautioned his mother.

CHAPTER XV

TIDINGS

The following week brought a letter from Uncle Frederick and very important the McGregors felt when they took it, adorned with its English stamp, from the mail box in the hall. Mulberry Court did not receive so many letters that the arrival of one was a routine affair. No, indeed! When a real letter came to any of its residents the fact was remarked upon by the recipient with a casualness calculated to veil the pride he or she experienced.

Mrs. O'Dowd, for example, in passing through the hall would call carelessly to one of her neighbors:

"I've just had a letter from my sister Jane in Fall River. Plague the girl! What can she be writing to me about?"

Nevertheless, in spite of this ungracious observation Mrs. O'Dowd was much pleased to be seen with the letter and over-hear her friends whispering among themselves:

"Julie O'Dowd had a letter from Jane to-day. It was in a blue envelope and looked like quite a thick one. What do you suppose the girl had to say? Most likely Julie will tell us by and by."

And sure enough! The prediction was a true prophecy, for before the day was out Julie had made an errand to every flat in the house and before leaving had read to each family extracts from the letter, interspersing the paragraphs with a running line of comment concerning Jane and her history since baby-hood. By evening the letter had become blurred and dingy with much handling and Julie could recite it from beginning to end.

Yet for all the interest evoked by Julie's letters and the other rare epistles that found their way into Mulberry Court these missives came after all only from American cities which lay within a radius of a hundred miles of Baileyville. They had not traveled far, any more than had the persons to whom they were addressed. They were not letters written on thin foreign paper and bearing unfamiliar postmarks and the fascinating stamps of other nations. Only the McGregors could boast such splendor as that.

Realizing this, Mrs. McGregor would have been short of human if she had not been a wee bit self-conscious and forced to suppress from her voice the satisfaction that echoed in it when she observed in off-hand fashion:

"Oh, by the way, I had a letter to-day from my brother who is in China."

China! It was a name to conjure with. What a medley of visions it brought to the imagination!

And if you could not go to China, as none of Mulberry Court ever expected to do, think of having a relative who did! And if you were not blessed with such an illustrious connection why the next best thing was to know some one who was. Even to know some one who had a brother in China and who sent home letters from that magic realm imparted a certain glory.

There was no denying the McGregors' foreign correspon-dence lent prestige to Mulberry Court. Perhaps a Manila post-mark was cut out and bestowed on Mrs. Murphy, who tucked it away in a cracked cup and displayed it on occasions to a visitor; or maybe the letter heading from a Genoa hotel was given to

Mrs. O'Dowd and furnished her with conversation for a week. In outbursts of great generosity stamps or postcards were donated to especially favored individuals.

Hence when on this particular morning the postman pressed Mrs. McGregor's bell and she hastened down four flights to open her mail-box a head protruded from almost every door as she made her way back upstairs and there was ample opportunity for her to observe to interested spectators, "I seem to have a letter from England. Judging from the postmark, my brother must be in Liverpool."

In this case the admiration with which the name was repeated might not have found so ringing an echo in Mrs. McGregor's voice. She had been to Liverpool. For all that, however, she maintained a dignified front and bore the letter upstairs, sinking with delight into the first chair that blocked her path when she arrived and calling to her children:

"I've a letter from your Uncle Frederick, Timmie. Think of that! It comes all the way from Liverpool with King George neat as a pin smiling out of the corner of it. Yes, you may take the envelope, Carl, but don't let the baby be fingering and tearing it. Show Martin the King's picture. He's old enough now to learn how he looks. Mercy on us! What a ream your Uncle Frederick has written. One would think it was a book! I never knew him to write such a long letter in all my life. I hope he isn't sick. Don't hang over my shoulder, Mary; it makes me nervous. And don't let Nell come climbing up into my lap while I'm reading. Go to Mary, like a good girl, darling; mother's reading a letter that came all the way from England."

Thus did Mrs. McGregor preface the perusal of the document she held in her hand. But when she had spread out the voluminous sheets and was preparing to read them she was again interrupted:

"Now, Timmie, don't you and Carl start quarreling the first thing about the stamp. You ought to be ashamed of yourselves. Who had the last one? Carl? Then this one goes to you and there must be no more bickering about it. If there is I shall keep it myself. One would think you boys were a pair of Kilkenny cats the way you squabble with each other! Now are you going to be quiet and listen to what Uncle Frederick has to say or are you not? Then don't let me hear another yip out of either of you."

Instantly the room was so still you could have heard a pin drop and to an accompaniment of crisply crackling paper Mrs. McGregor began:

Liverpool, January 29, 1924.

Dear Sister Nellie—,

Well, here I am in England with the Atlantic rolling between me and Baileyville. We had a splendid voyage with the sea as smooth as the top of your sewing-machine. (Ain't that like your Uncle Frederick to joke about the ocean! He's crossed it that number of times it's no more to him than the pond in the park. Well, I'm glad he had a smooth trip, anyway.)

At Liverpool, where we docked, we ran into our first trouble, for there was a longshoremen's strike on and not a soul could he found to unload our cargo or lend a hand in loading us up again. For three days we were tied plumb to the wharf with nothing to do but twirl our thumbs. So having business at Manchester I decided to go up there and stay with a Scotchman who was my first mate years ago. (Now wasn't that nice!) Old Barney turned the town inside out he was so glad to see me (I'll wager he was!) and among other things took me through some big cotton mills where a nephew of his was working. For the benefit of the children I'm going to write a bit about them. I could not but wish on top of what we all talked about that they might have been with me to see how wonderful the spinning machinery is. Were it actually alive it could not work with more brains. (Your Uncle Frederick always will have his joke!)

Indeed, the man who took us about told me that the self-acting mule of to-day, founded on the invention of Crompton, is a product of hundreds of minds and I can well believe it. It isn't the principle that is new, for apparently no one has ever improved on Crompton's idea; but since that time this machinist and that has added his bit to make the device more perfect. (Now ain't you glad you read about Crompton, Carl? This letter would have been Greek to you if you hadn't.) We saw mules as long as a hundred and twenty feet, and from nine to ten feet wide carrying some twelve or thirteen hundred spindles, and turning out about two yards of thread in a quarter of a minute. How is that? And all this clicking, humming, whirling machinery was operated by a man and a couple of boys. Carl, Tim and I could have run the thing had we known how.

(Your Uncle Frederick don't forget you boys, you see!)

They told me it was Richard Roberts, a Manchester man, who in 1830 improved the self-acting mule and brought it to its present state of practical working order. I take off my hat to him and to those on whose ideas he built up this marvelous invention. The thing does everything but talk, and maybe it's as well off without doing that. Lots of folks would be.

(I must read Julie O'Dowd that; it will make her laugh. It sounds so like your uncle you'd think him in the room this minute.)

It draws out the carded cotton, puts in the necessary twist, and spins the thread, easy as rolling off a log, levers, wheels, springs, and a friction clutch all doing their part. I couldn't help thinking if each of us humans played his rôle as well, and did the thing given him to do as faithfully, how much better a world we should have. We don't begin to pull together for a result the way those wheels and pulleys did. Instead, each of us goes his own way never cooperating with his neighbor and in consequence we have a helter-skelter universe. (How true that is!)

Nevertheless in spite of us—not because of us—the world advances. I sometimes wonder how it does it. Crompton, for instance, would scarcely have recognized his old mule that gave subsequent inventors their inspiration. Nor would Arkwright know his water frame could he see what has happened to it. (Mark you, Carl, how he speaks of Arkwright. All that would slide off you hadn't you read that book!)

Of course there is a lot of rivalry between English and American spinning machinery and I found that some of the mills here have both.

The reeling of the yarn after it is spun is done chiefly by women. I do not mean they make it up into skeins by hand; they operate the machinery that winds it; also that which makes it up into packages for the market. This process is also interesting to see. Strings are put in to separate the laps of the yarn; cardboards hold it in place; it is pressed flat; the bundle is tied; and the paper wrapper bearing the name of the manufacturer as well as any printed advertising he wishes to circulate, is whisked about it.

I was a little surprised to find they made no spool cotton on any of these machines. Up to date no machine has been invented that will directly spin thread strong enough for sewing. All that has to be a separate process and therefore the yarn is taken to other machines where it is drawn finer and where several of the fine threads can be twisted into one. The spinners know just how many fine threads to put together to get certain sizes of cotton. To make number twelve, for example, they put together four strands of what is called 48's that have been doubled, or perhaps 50's, since the twist contracts the yarn.

After this has been twisted the proper number of times the thread is passed over flannel-covered boards to be cleaned. Next it travels through a small, round hole something like the eye of a needle so that any knots or rough places can be detected. If the threads are found to be strong and without flaws two to half a dozen of them are put together in a loose skein and they are twisted in a doubling machine. Afterward the thread is polished, cleaned, and run off on spools or bobbins. That is the road Mother's spools of cotton have to travel before they get to her. How seldom we think of this or are grateful for it!

There are in addition other ways of preparing cottons for embroidery, crocheting, or knitting, not to mention methods used to finish cotton yarn so that it will look like woolen, linen, or silk fiber. Because cotton is a cheaper material than any of these it is often mixed with them to produce cheaper goods. You would be amazed to see how ingenious manufacturers have become in turning out such imitations. Cotton, for example, is mercerized by passing it very rapidly through a gassing machine not unlike the flame of a Bunsen burner. Here all the fuzz protruding from it is burned away, and when polished and finished it looks so much like silk you would have trouble in telling whether it was or not. This sort of yarn is used to make imitation silk stockings and many other articles.

Now I have told you quite a story, haven't I? And no doubt I have wasted good ink and paper doing it, for I presume Hal Harling could have told you the same thing quite as well if not a deal better. You read him this document and ask him to fill in the gaps. But at least even if Hal can improve on my tale I have demonstrated one thing and that is that I have remembered you whenever I have seen anything I thought you would be interested in.

I send much love to each of the family. Tell Mary, Carl, and Tim to take good care of Mother and the babies. Be sure to greet for me the Harlings, O'Dowds, Murphys, and all the neighbors at Mulberry Court. We leave Liverpool for the Mediterranean next week and I will write you from Gibraltar or Naples. In the meantime do not forget the good ship *Charlotte* or your affectionate

FREDERICK.

"As if we could forget him!" whispered Mrs. McGregor, folding up the many sheets and replacing them in their envelope. "It isn't all children that have the kind uncle you have. Carl, maybe you'd like to be stepping over to the Harlings with this letter. Grandfather Harling would delight to read it, I know. The days are long ones for him and I'm sure he must miss your Uncle Frederick dropping in to bring him the news."

Only too ready to comply with her request Carl rose.

"You can leave the letter until they all have seen it; then Hal or Louise can bring it back. I want Mrs. O'Dowd to have it next. She's mentioned by name in it and it will please her to read the words herself."

Thus did Mulberry Court share its blessings!

CHAPTER XVI

A RELUCTANT ALTRUIST

As spring came and Carl was more out of doors playing ball and tramping the open country, his watchful eyes were continually scanning passing motors for a possible glimpse of the mysterious red racing car and its genial owner. The boy had never forgotten this delightful stranger or quite abandoned the hope that he might sometime see him again. But, alas, day succeeded day and never did any of the fleeting vehicles his glance followed contain the person he sought. Neither was the search for the sender of the Christmas baskets rewarded.

Spasmodically since mid-winter the Harlings and McGregors had cudgeled their brains to discover this elusive good fairy until at length, exhausted by fruitless effort, they agreed to inter Louise's philanthropic Mr. X in a nameless grave. Despite that fact, however, he was not forgotten and tender thoughts clustered about his memory.

In the meantime May followed on April's heels and presently June, with her greenery and wealth of roses arrived, and then the startling tidings buzzed through Baileyville that Mr. John Coulter was to be married. The news thrilled young and old alike for was not young Mr. Coulter the junior partner of Davis and Coulter; and was not Davis and Coulter the heart and soul of Baileyville? Davis and Coulter meant the mills and the mills meant the town itself. Without them there would have been no village at all. Boys and girls, men and women toiled year in and year out in the factories as their fathers and mothers, often their grandfathers and grandmothers had done before them. If you were not connected with Davis and Coulter's you were not of Baileyville's aristocracy.

Hence it followed that the prospective marriage of Mr. John Coulter could not but be an event concerning which the entire community gossiped with eager and kindly interest. The lady was from New York, people said, and Mr. John had met her while doing war work in France. Both of them had large fortunes. But the fact that appealed to the villagers far more than this was the intelligence that the wedding was to take place at the old Coulter homestead and be followed by a fête to which all the mill people and their families were to be invited. How exciting that was! And how exultant were those whose connection with the mills insured them a card to this mammoth festivity!

Rumor whispered there were to be gigantic tents with games and dancing; bands of music; fireworks; and every imaginable dainty to eat. Some even went so far as to assert there would be boats on the miniature lake and a Punch and Judy show. Oh, it was to be a fête indeed!

For weeks the town talked of nothing else; and as Carl McGregor listened to these stories his regrets at not being numbered among Davis and Coulter's elect waxed keener and keener. One did not enjoy being left out of a function of such magnitude, a party to which everybody else was going. Not only did it make you feel lonely and stranded but it mortified you to be obliged to own you were not of the happy band included in so magnificent a celebration.

"Now if you'd only have let me take a job at the mills as I wanted to, Ma, we might have been going to Mr. Coulter's party along with the rest of the world," Carl bemoaned. "I always told you I ought to go into those mills the way the other fellows do. But you wouldn't hear to it. Now see what's come of it. We are left high and dry. I'll bet we are the only people in Baileyville who are not invited to that party. Everybody is to be there. If even one member of a family works at the mill that lets in the bunch."

"Like the garden parties great families used to give their tenants in the old country," Mrs. McGregor murmured reminiscently.

"I don't know about the old country," replied Carl ungraciously, "but that is what Mr. Coulter is going to do—ask whole families. Gee, but it makes me sore!"

"If your father had lived we would have been there," said the boy's mother sadly. "Your father used to be very good friends with old Mr. Coulter and he would have seen to it that none of this household was left out. But Mr. John we never knew. He was always away studying—first at school, then at college, and then in Europe. Later he started in to be a lawyer in New York and but for the war and his father's death he'd most likely be doing that now. But when the old gentleman died Mr. John gave up everything else and came home to take his place in the firm as his father had wished he should. Folks say that in spite of not caring much for the mills at first he has persisted at his job until he has become genuinely interested in them. I honor him for it, too, for a business life wasn't his real choice. Of course being away so much as he has he is little known among the mill people yet; but evidently he means to settle down here and is anxious to get better acquainted. This wedding party shows that."

"Well, there are some he won't get acquainted with," lamented Carl.

"If you mean us I reckon he can worry along without," Mrs. McGregor retorted, with a twinkle in her eye. "He's managed to up to now."

"We're just as good as anybody else," her son blazed.

"Undoubtedly we are," was the good-humored answer. "Nevertheless we won't be missed in a crowd like that."

"Don't you *want* to go to the party, Ma?"

"Why, to tell the truth, I haven't had time to think much about it, sonny—that is, not to be disappointed. I'm not pretending, though, that so many parties come my way that a fine one such as this wouldn't be a treat. I can't remember the day I've been to anything of the sort. It's a quarter of a century or more, certainly—not since I was a girl and went to the balls the gentry gave in Scotland."

"Oh, I do so wish we were going to Mr. Coulter's," Carl repeated.

"I'll not deny I'd like to," confessed his mother a bit wistfully. "Still, were we to go what a stew we'd be in! It would mean days of washing and ironing; new neckties and maybe shoes for you boys; and hair ribbons and folderols for Mary and Nell. Before we were all properly equipped it would cost a pretty penny. We'd have no right to go without looking decent and being a credit to your father and to Mr. Coulter who was good enough to ask us. So, you see, there are advantages in everything. If we are not invited we shall have none of the trouble and expense of it," concluded the woman philosophically.

"I wouldn't mind the trouble, Mother," burst out Carl. "I wouldn't even care if I didn't have new shoes. Why, I'd go in my bathing suit."

Nodding her head his mother regarded him with withering censure.

"Yes, I believe you would," she agreed, "I believe you would—if you were permitted. But how lucky it is you have a mother. Without me you'd be disgracing your name, Mr. Coulter, Baileyville, and Mulberry Court."

Carl grinned in sickly fashion.

"I'd be having the time of my life!" announced he, undaunted.

"Going to an affair like that in your bathing suit, you mean? I'm not so sure about that. You are always begging to be allowed to wear that costume or grumbling because you cannot wear it. Once, I recall, you actually suggested wearing it to church on a hot Sunday. I'm sorely tempted sometime to let you have your way and see what would come of it. Think, for instance, of your sailing into Mr. John Coulter's wedding party in a get-up like that. You'd be ducked in the pond in a second."

"I'd be ready for it," was the provoking answer.

"Well, you aren't going to the Coulter party, as it happens, so there'll be no question of what you'll wear," returned Mrs. McGregor grimly.

"I know I'm not; but you don't have to rub it in, Ma," Carl answered.

"I didn't mean to rub it in, dear," was the gentle response. "I was merely stating facts. Maybe it's as well, too, that we're not going ourselves, for with the Sullivans, Murphys, and O'Dowds all invited we'll have as much as we can do to get them all creditably rigged out. I shall let Julie wear my black skirt—it just fits her; and Mrs. Sullivan my best hat. My waist Mrs. Murphy shall take if I can get it washed in time. Most likely, too, the O'Dowds will need your clothes and Timmie's."

"Need my clothes!" Carl shouted.

"Certainly. Julie can't hope to provide things for all that big family to appear in at once. Somebody will have to turn to and lend a helping hand."

"But what'll I do while the O'Dowd boys wear my clothes?" wailed Carl.

"Why, you can stay in the house. It won't hurt either you or Tim to take an afternoon of rest," came stoically from his mother.

"But I don't want to take an afternoon of rest," Carl protested wrathfully. "Not on that day of all others. I'm going up to Coulters to hang round outside and watch the fun. If I'm not invited I can at least do that."

"Carl McGregor! You'll do nothing of the sort. Hang round outside, indeed! Haven't you any pride at all? If you're not asked to the party I should hope you'd have the good taste to keep out of the way of it. Hang round outside! You ought to be ashamed even to suggest such a thing," said Mrs. McGregor with scorn. "No, you'll do no lingering on the outskirts of Mr. John's reception, you can make up your mind to that. You'll stay politely at home as the rest of us plan to do and keep under cover so folks won't be asking you why you're not up at Coulters. I've some regard for the family dignity if you haven't. And since you'll be at home anyway, you may as well take the chance to do a kindly deed and let Frankie O'Dowd wear your clothes. You don't want to grow up to be selfish."

"My pants will be miles too long for that O'Dowd kid," responded the unwilling altruist grudgingly.

"Oh, his mother can baste them up so they'll do for one afternoon," was the serene answer.

"Huh! I don't envy Frank going to that party with two thicknesses of trousers on his legs," Carl declared. "If it's a hot day he'll melt."

"Beggars cannot be choosers," Mrs. McGregor asserted. "Likely Frankie will be that tickled to go to the lawn party that he won't care what he has on any more than you would. You'd go quicker than a wink in basted-up trousers if you got the chance."

"You bet I would! Why, I'd go in—in—in *anything!*" was the fervent affirmation. "Somehow, Ma, it just seems as if I couldn't give up the idea of going. I feel as if something *must* happen so we'd get asked."

"Why, Carl—you silly boy! You don't mean to say you are actually cherishing the thought you may be invited yet?" his mother exclaimed incredulously. "Put it out of your head, son, like a sensible lad. There isn't a chance of it, dear. The invitations were sent out last week and had you been going to get one you would have received it days ago. There'll be no more people asked now."

"There might be—some might have been forgotten by mistake. Or the invitation might have got stuck in the letter box and delayed."

"I'm afraid not, Carlie!" his mother said gently. "Mark my words, all the invitations there are going to be to that garden party have gone out. There won't be any more. The folks that haven't had theirs already won't have none and if you're wise you will face that fact and give up thinking about Mr. Coulter and his wedding."

The corners of Carl's mouth drooped but he stubbornly insisted:

"Well, anyhow, Ma, don't you tell Frankie O'Dowd he can have my clothes until the very last minute, will you? Promise me that."

"Aye! I'll not mention the clothes yet awhile. I'll wait at least a day or two. Most likely Julie or the Murphys will be up by that time and ask for 'em."

And with this scanty comfort Carl was obliged to be content.

Even the concession that he would be allowed to wear his bathing suit while at home was but feeble consolation. What did it matter what he wore if he couldn't go to the Coulter fête?

CHAPTER XVII

AN ORDEAL

As the date for the Coulters' fête approached the weather was breathlessly scanned in practically every home in Baileyville and throbbing hearts almost ceased to beat lest the day be stormy or too cold to wear the finery that awaited the great occasion. Could one have taken off the roofs of the houses between his thumb and forefinger as he would lift the cover off a sugar-bowl, what a bewildering array of freshly starched muslins, clean shirts and collars, shining shoes, and rose-encircled hats would have met his gaze!

Carl McGregor had spoken truly when he had affirmed to his mother that everybody in the town was going to the wedding festival. All Baileyville was on tiptoe with excitement. The schools were to be closed for the afternoon, not alone to do Mr. Coulter honor, but because it was quite evident that no children would be found in their seats on the great day.

"We McGregors would be the only kids in the whole place, I bet, if they did have school," declared Carl gloomily. "You see, Ma, it's just as I told you—everybody's going to the Coulters'."

"I should think, hating school as you do, you'd be thankful to have a holiday," commented Mary.

"Ordinarily I would," was the prompt reply. "But what good is this holiday going to do me, I'd like to know, with Frankie

O'Dowd wearing all my clothes, and Mother forbidding me to go out of the house in my bathing suit?"

"Well, at least you won't have to study," said his optimistic sister, making an effort to comfort her morose companion.

"I might as well study; it would take up my mind," fretted Carl. "I've nothing better to do."

His ill humor was so tragic that in spite of herself Mary laughed.

"Well, you needn't grin so over it, Miss Superiority, or go pretending you don't wish you could go to the lawn party."

"Of course I'd love to go," Mary confessed honestly. "But if we can't I don't see any use in mourning about it and talking of nothing else."

"I *have* to talk about it. I think of it every minute."

"Put it out of your head."

"I can't."

"Nonsense! You don't try. Why don't you set about doing something and forget it instead of sitting round mooning and working yourself all up? You can run down and get the mail right now. There's the bell. Maybe it's a letter from Uncle Frederick."

Welcoming the diversion her brother rose with alacrity. He was in a mood when any excitement, no matter how trivial, was a boon. Down the stairs he ran only to return a second later with a square white envelope in his hand.

"Is it from Uncle Frederick?" queried Mary eagerly.

"Nope!"

"Oh, I'm sorry, we haven't heard from him for ever so long. I do hope nothing's the matter. Who is the letter from?"

"I don't know."

Something in the reticence of the reply caused the girl to glance up.

"I'll take it in to Mother," volunteered she, holding out her hand.

"It isn't for Mother," Carl answered slowly.

"Not for Mother? How funny! None of the rest of us ever have letters. Who is it for?"

"It happens to be mine."

"Carl!" Dismay and apprehension vibrated in the word.

"Yes, it's mine," her brother repeated. His obvious attempt to carry off the episode in jaunty fashion failed, however, and it was evident by his tense tones that he echoed Mary's alarm.

"But who on earth can be writing to you?" demanded his sister.

"I—I—don't know." The boy fingered the envelope with uneasiness. Mary came nearer.

"Carl, what have you been up to now?" asked she. "That looks like the teacher's writing. Aren't you going to be promoted or what is the matter?"

"How do I know until I read the thing?" snapped Carl.

"You're not in any scrape?"

"Not that I know of."

"Honestly?"

"I tell you I can't think of any. On my honor I can't."

"Oh, well then, it's probably about your work. Most likely you're behind the class in something and Miss Dewey wants to see you. Why don't you buck up and find out what she has to say?"

"I'm going to in a minute."

"You're afraid to open that letter. You've done something at school you don't want Mother and me to know about."

"I tell you I haven't."

"Then why, for pity's sake, don't you read what Miss Dewey

has written instead of looking at the note as if it was a bomb? Maybe she's inviting you to supper. She does ask the boys sometimes."

This possibility was so encouraging that the startled expression in the lad's eyes gave place to a serener light. Perhaps after all the missive did not portend the calamity that a note from school usually did. Maybe his algebra was all right and he had not flunked his Latin. The fates may have graciously intervened.

Courageously he tore open the envelope; then a sharp cry came from his lips.

"Hurrah!" he cried. "Mother! Mother! Where are you?"

"Here, dear, in my room. Is anything the matter?"

Carl rushed off unceremoniously, leaving the mystified Mary alone in the middle of the kitchen.

"Oh, Ma," he panted, "what do you suppose? We're going, after all—every one of us! Think of it! We're going!"

"Going where? Have you taken leave of your senses, sonny? What are you talking about, pray?"

"We're going to the Coulters', Ma," asserted Carl, waving the white envelope above his head in a frenzy of delight. "Look! Here's the bid. And across the bottom of the paper Mr. Coulter himself has written to say that he's sorry the invitation has been so delayed and he hopes my mother and all of us—even the baby—will come. Gee!"

Quite exhausted, Carl dropped into a chair.

"But why should Mr. Coulter send this invitation to you?"

"I don't know, I'm sure. Maybe Hal Harling or somebody told him how disappointed I was at not being asked," returned Carl serenely.

"Mercy! I hope not," ejaculated his horrified mother.

"Why not?"

"Why, it would be almost like asking Mr. Coulter for an invitation."

"He wouldn't care, I guess," came comfortably from Carl. "There's plenty of room and there'll be food enough so a few people more or less wouldn't bother him."

"But I wouldn't think of going to a party, or letting you, if you had demanded in so many words to be invited," returned Mrs. McGregor with a toss of her head.

"You don't mean to say, Ma, that you're thinking of not going," her son gasped.

"I certainly shall not stir a step to Mr. Coulter's until I find out how we happened to receive this remarkable invitation."

"Ma!"

"I sha'n't," repeated his mother. "Why, the bare idea of your trying to get a card to that wedding reception!"

"I didn't try to, Mother; honest, I didn't," protested Carl. "I didn't ask anybody to do a thing for me. I was only fooling when I said that. Of course Hal Harling knows well enough that I've been crazy to go. He and Louise couldn't help seeing how sore I was about it. But I never said anything else."

"I'm thankful to hear that. One never knows what you will do."

Mrs. McGregor gave a sigh of relief and taking the card examined it.

"Perhaps," she presently observed in a gentler tone, "this invitation has nothing to do with you. It may be possible that young Mr. Coulter remembered how long your father worked in the mills and thought it would be nice to ask us because of that. If so, it was very thoughtful of him. And most likely the card was sent to you because he happened to have heard your name. Goodness knows, with the messes you're in, I should think all the town might be aware of it."

"And you'll go, Ma?" In his eagerness Carl brushed aside the unflattering picture his mother's words presented.

"If I find it's a bona fide invitation and not some of your concocting I'll go—not otherwise. It would be ungrateful to snub Mr. John if he is trying to be kind. But the thing that makes me doubtful is that the envelope should be addressed to you. Why wasn't the invitation sent to me? I am the head of the family—or at least I attempt to be," amended she with an upward curve of her lips.

"Oh, who cares, Ma, who the invitation was addressed to?" cut in Carl impatiently. "The main thing is that it's come and we are going to the party. I'd go had it been sent to James Frederick. What does it matter? Say, Ma, isn't it lucky you hadn't loaned our clothes? We'll need 'em ourselves now."

"When is the wedding?" Mary asked.

"Do you mean to say you don't even know?" inquired her brother with scorn.

"I've forgotten."

"You have! Then you are the only person in Baileyville who has," was the sarcastic rejoinder. "Well, if you must know, it's the day after to-day."

"It will be a scramble to get ready, won't it, Mother?" commented the practical Mary.

"There certainly will be a lot to do," Mrs. McGregor agreed. "However, I guess we can manage if everybody will turn to."

"I'll help," announced Carl in a burst of magnanimousness. "I'll wash and iron all my own clothes."

"I'd like a peep at the shirt you washed and ironed," taunted Mary in derision.

"I fancy a peep would be enough," put in her mother, laughing. "No, son, your talent does not lie in washing or ironing.

But you can take care of the youngsters while Mary and I do it. And, Mary, we'll have to get a bunch of fresh flowers for your best hat; those pink daisies are too faded to wear. We'll get a new hair ribbon, too. And I must have some other lace in the neck of my silk waist and——"

"Oh, if you're going to talk ribbon, artificial flowers, and all that rot I'm going over to Harlings," announced Carl, rising.

"Indeed you're not," objected his mother. "You're going to get out the blacking bottle and start cleaning and polishing the shoes. There'll be seven pairs to get ready and I want a fine shine on every one of them."

"But what's the use of doing it now? They'll get all dusty again before the day after to-morrow," Carl grumbled.

"Not if they're put away," came in even accents from his mother. "We'll just have to wear slippers, sneakers and things until Tuesday. I guess we can get along. We can't go leaving everything until the last minute or we shall be all up in a heap. We must begin directly to get things done. I shall braid your hair, Mary, and Nell's right away, so it will be well crimped. And Timmie, you and Carl and Martin have all got to have baths. Yes, you have, whether you like it or not. If you don't you can't go. That's all there is about that, so stop fussing. Carl, you put some kettles of water on the stove to heat. You boys must be scrubbed whether the rest of us are or not. You need it most. And Mary, run like a good girl and see if you can hunt up a clean pair of stockings for everybody—stockings without too many holes. Mercy on us! I wish Mr. Coulter had given us a little more notice—indeed I do!"

"I don't see who's going to know, in that push, whether I've had a bath or not," persisted the argumentative Tim.

"You don't? Have you happened to get a glimpse of that ebony ring round your neck?" interrogated his mother significantly. "Anybody who saw that would have some notion."

"I hate a bath!"

"You look it."

"Oh, shut up, Timmie," cautioned Carl in an undertone. "Don't go rowing at Ma now. If you do she may get her back up and not take you to the party at all. I hate to be scrubbed within an inch of my life as much as you do, but I'm not saying so to-day. I'd be boiled in oil sooner than not go to this party. Besides, your neck is black. I'll bet it will take sapolio to get it clean. But don't go yammering about it. Just hop and do as Ma tells you. It's the only way."

Heeding the wisdom of his elder brother Tim ceased further protests and *hopped.*

Indeed the hopping became very spirited and general during the short interval that preceded the wedding day. And when at last that glorious morning dawned cloudless and fair, what a scarlet, shining, spotless cavalcade of McGregors its radiant light shone upon!

First there was Mrs. McGregor, hot but triumphant in a petticoat that crackled like brittle ice beneath her black alpaca skirt and a pair of white cotton gloves at the fingers of which she was continually tugging. Both her hat and Mary's gleamed ebon under a recent coat of blacking—so recent that they entertained some concern lest it trickle down their heated faces in disfiguring rivulets. Mary's white dress rustled as crisply as did her mother's petticoat and her hair, crimped and ironed until it was fuzzy as a bushman's, drifted out behind her, a hempen whirlwind. New flowers on her hat and accompanying pink streamers afforded her tranquil satisfaction as did also the string of coral beads Uncle Frederick had once sent from Naples, a gift worn only on very special occasions.

As for the boys, every hair of their heads had been plastered securely into place, and blistered with scrubbing, they stood wretched but hopeful in a row waiting with patience the moment when clean shirts, creased trousers, and sparkling boots might be forgotten in the delights the Coulter party promised.

Even Nell and the baby looked unnatural and reflected the general discomfort and self-consciousness.

The getting-ready had been a fatiguing ordeal and everybody's nerves were at the breaking point. Systematically Mrs. McGregor had proceeded with the process, beginning with the eldest of the family, and as each work of art was completed it was set aside much as a frosted cake is set away to cool, and the next victim was summoned.

In the meantime those who had been *finished*, motionless in chairs, were allowed the entertainment of watching each succeeding martyr put through his round of torture. Yet diverting as this had been, the waiting had been tedious, particularly for those who stood at the head of the line.

Now, the rite over, everybody drew a long breath and struggled to forget past miseries. Therefore when Hal and Louise Harling, who were to augment the procession, arrived, every cloud was put to flight and the delegation set forth in the highest of spirits.

"What a pity it is Uncle Frederick Dillingham isn't here!" commented Mrs. McGregor, as they went along. "And what a shame, too, that Grandfather Harling and your mother, Louise, cannot see this day! It would furnish them with something to talk of for weeks."

"Hal and I will tell them all about it," returned the girl brightly. "Isn't it splendid you all could go? Poor Carl was so disappointed when he thought he was to be out of it."

"I know he was," nodded the lad's mother. "In fact, it worried me not a little lest it was because he made his disappointment so evident that we got invited. I was afraid some well-meaning person might have taken pity on him and begged him a card. Had not you and Hal declared you had nothing to do with our being asked, I should not have stirred a peg to the party, let Carl plead as he might. But now I feel more comfortable about our going, although I must confess it puzzles me why the invitation was sent to him instead of to me. It certainly seems a little funny. However, it may have been an accident. Of course Mr. Coulter has had a lot to think of and might well be forgiven one mistake. It isn't likely he could remember my husband's name. He was pretty good to think of us at all."

"They say at the mills that Mr. John is very friendly and has ever so many plans afoot for the workers. There is even talk of a recreation building being put up on the factory grounds."

"Not much like his father, who wouldn't spend a cent he didn't have to," mused Mrs. McGregor.

"No. Mr. John is different; everybody says so. Besides, he is younger and belongs to a generation with other ideas."

"Better ideas, I hope. If children didn't improve on their fathers where would the world be?" Then suddenly cutting short her philosophical meditations Mrs. McGregor called imperatively:

"Timmie, stop chasing those butterflies this minute. Do you want to spoil the shine on your shoes before you even get to the party? You'll have your collar ruined if you gallop round and get so hot. Come back here and walk beside me. I'm resolved to land you all at Mr. Coulter's looking like human beings, whatever happens afterward. Then if you prefer to smooch your face with dirt and rumple up your hair, I can't help it. But you shall stay clean until you're inside the gate."

Glaring for a moment on her subjects with subduing ferocity Mrs. McGregor drew herself up and moved majestically in at the entrance of the Coulter mansion.

CHAPTER XVIII

THE SOLUTION OF MANY MYSTERIES

Once inside the magic portal of the great estate, however, Mrs. McGregor's task became increasingly difficult. What a bewildering scene it was! The green lawns, terraced down to the lake, were dotted with tents and from each one floated out tantalizing hints of the delights within. The strains of a band and the laughter of dancers drifted forth from one; waiters with heavily laden trays passed in and out of another; around still a third swarmed children and one glimpsed through the open doorway a marionette show. Under a gay red umbrella at the edge of the garden women, fluttering like multi-hued butterflies, ladled lemonade from giant punch-bowls.

Oh, a wonderland of myriad delights beckoned in every direction and it was only by dint of extreme severity that Mrs. McGregor succeeded in keeping her little army in formation and preventing its neatly ranged ranks from becoming lost in the surrounding hubbub.

"You're not to stir a step from this spot until I tell you you may," commanded she. "The very notion of your all racing off to enjoy yourselves before you have so much as said a word of thanks to Mr. Coulter who asked you here! Where are your manners? Are you forgetting so quick that it is his wedding

"I'VE HUNTED FOR YOU AND YOUR RED CAR EVER SINCE."

day? Aren't you going to wish him joy as is proper to do when he has taken all this trouble to give you a good time?"

Her tone was withering in its rebuke and as if hypnotized by its cadence the wriggling children thronging in her wake stood motionless.

"In my day folks were grateful for what was done for them and expected to say *thank you* to their elders. Now there seems to be no such thing as politeness among youngsters. But to-day, whether you will or no, before you do anything else we are going to hunt up Mr. John and his bride and every one of you is to thank him for asking you to his party. And Tim, you and Mary and Carl are to repeat the speech I taught you. I pray you've not forgotten it already. You hope he and his wife will have many days as happy as this one. Remember and don't get mixed up and say the wrong thing."

With this final caution Mrs. McGregor wheeled about and marshalled the miniature procession following her into a vast, rose-garlanded tent at the right of the entrance. Two aisles roped off with laurel divided it, and throngs of people were moving down one of these and returning by the other. In the far distance one could see a canopy of green, a figure misty in white tulle, and a bevy of bridesmaids in pink, blue, yellow, and lavender.

"This seems to be the right place," whispered Mrs. McGregor. "We'll fall right in behind this man and woman. Now mind your manners, all of you. Poor though we are, we can be polite without it costing us a cent. Timmie, you keep close at my heels with Mary. I've got all I can do to handle the baby and Nell. Carl, see that you don't squeeze Martin's hand too tight and get him peevish. Take hold of him gently. And don't one of you dare to push. We must expect to move along slowly and wait our turn. Yes, I know it's hot. But there'll be lemonade and ice cream by and by. I guess you can stand the heat for a little while. What is it, Tim? Your boots hurt? Nonsense! They're the same boots you always wear, aren't they? Were you racing round playing ball in them it's little notice you'd be taking of them, I reckon. Don't be silly and get sulky now or next time I shall leave you at home."

To an accompaniment of these and similar admonitions the McGregor host proceeded on its way along with the other guests.

Then at last when the receiving party was well in sight and Mrs. McGregor and her family were making a decorous approach the anxious mother was horrified to see Carl, forgetful of all else, rush from the line and racing up to Mr. John Coulter, seize both his hands.

"Oh!" cried the boy, in a voice so shrill with ecstasy that its accents penetrated to every corner of the great tent, "Oh, Mr. Coulter, I never dreamed it was you! Why didn't you tell me who you were? I'm so glad to see you again! I thought I never would. I've hunted and hunted for you and your red car ever since."

Plainly Mr. John Coulter, instead of being offended by this unexpected onslaught, was delighted for he beamed down on the excited lad, shook both his hands heartily, and laughed so the ring of it echoed all about.

"So you didn't guess the riddle, little chap," Mrs. McGregor heard him say. "Well, I didn't mean you should."

"And to think it was you!" Carl was still murmuring, as if in a trance. "Just to think it was you! Of course you were the one who got Louise her new place."

"Guilty."

"Gee, but it was white of you! She's right here behind my mother." Then inspired by sudden understanding he added, "And the Christmas dinners came from you, too."

"Come, come, youngster, this is no moment to be confronting me with all my crimes," the blushing bridegroom protested. "Here's Mrs. Coulter just married to me—what is she going to think if you tell her how many conspiracies I have been mixed up in? This, Marion, is one of my very good friends, Carl McGregor. His father was for many years in our mills and if I mistake not here is his whole family coming up to speak to us."

"Indeed we are, sir," declared Mrs. McGregor, making a quaint English curtsy, "and it's scandalized enough I am to see my boy here racing at you as if he was a wild beast and forgetting all the etiquette I've taught him. He had a nice speech ready to say but where it is now heaven only knows!"

"I'd far rather he said to me what he did," asserted Mr. Coulter. "You see, Carl and I are old friends."

"I don't see," replied the mystified mother, "but no doubt you are, since you tell me so. I myself had no idea the lad know you from Adam."

"And I hadn't either, Mother. Gee, but it is rich! To think I went riding with you that day, Mr. Coulter, and speeled off all that guff, and you never so much as raised an eyelash!"

"Carl!" ejaculated his despairing parent.

"Well, I hope this is not to be the end of our acquaintance, youngster," Mr. Coulter returned, passing over Mrs. McGregor's rebuke. "Come and see Mrs. Coulter and me some day. And remember that if you ever wish to enter the mills I will make a place for you."

"That's bully of you, sir!"

"Carl!" Mrs. McGregor was dumb with consternation. "The very idea of your speaking to Mr. Coulter like that!" declared she, when at last she could catch her breath. "Come away before you say anything more to disgrace the family. There's others waiting to give him their good wishes and you seem to have forgotten all about yours, although goodness knows you were drilled and drilled on the speech you were to make. Yes, Mrs. Coulter, these are my children—all six of them. The baby's name? James Frederick, after his uncle. And this is Mary, and Timmie, and Martin, and Nell. The oldest ones had nice things ready to say to you but Carl has knocked 'em clean out of their heads. I hope you'll not lay it up against us. No, marm, this tall boy and girl don't belong to me, but I'm that fond of 'em I wish they did. They are our neighbors, Hal and Louise Harling."

Instantly Mr. Coulter reached forward and greeted the young people.

"The new job is going well?" he asked, addressing Louise.

"Oh, I'm so happy in it, Mr. Coulter."

"That's good! And you, Harling?"

"I'm getting on splendidly, sir."

"Excellent! There'll be a raise coming to you next month—quite a substantial one. We've been looking you up."

"Oh, sir, how can I——"

"There, there! We mustn't stop to talk about it now. If you must thank somebody for it thank this young scoundrel here. It was he put me up to it."

There was time for nothing further. Swept onward by crowds that surged behind, the McGregors, like chips on the crest of a mammoth wave, were borne forward and out of the tent.

In the open air Mrs. McGregor wiped her perspiring brow.

"Now," began she, turning accusingly on her son, "perhaps you will be so good as to tell us what all this is about. How came you to know Mr. John Coulter well enough to be treating him like a long-lost brother? And what had you to do with Hal and Louise and the Coulter mills? I feel as if I were going crazy! One minute you don't even know Mr. Coulter by sight and the next he is sending us a Christmas dinner and you are fairly falling on his neck."

Carl shook with laughter.

"Oh, Mother, it's all so rich—so perfectly corking!" he cried. "You couldn't half appreciate it if I told you."

"I could try," came curtly from Mrs. McGregor.

But her son did not heed her.

"To think of that being Mr. John Coulter," chuckled he. "And, oh, the things I said to him! I tremble to recall them. I told him Corcoran was a low-down skunk, I know that. And I gushed on a lot about Hal and Louise. I only wish I could remember what I did say. Jove! He must have split his sides laughing."

"When? When did you do all this?" interrogated the lad's mother impatiently.

"Oh, when was it?" ruminated Carl, struggling to collect his scattered wits. "It seems ages and ages ago that all that happened. It was before Christmas, I'm certain of that."

"And you went riding with Mr. Coulter? I heard you saying something about it."

"Yes."

"You actually went to ride with him?"

"I sure did!"

"Well, all I can say is I should like to know when all these miracles took place," repeated Carl's mother. "Where was I, and why wasn't I told? You might at least have mentioned it at home."

"I know it, Ma," apologized Carl with disarming frankness. "I did try twice to tell you but the chance never seemed to come right; and by and by it got to be so long ago that I forgot all about it."

"Forgot you went motoring with Mr. John Coulter?" Mrs. McGregor spoke with incredulity.

"You see I didn't know at the time that it was Mr. John Coulter, Ma."

"I don't see! I don't understand anything about it," repeated the woman helplessly.

"Well, you will by and by. It is a long story—too long to tell now. When we get home you shall hear it from beginning to end. But now—— Gee whizz! There goes Martin making for the pond! I'll head him off."

Away went Carl across the velvet lawn and with an unsatisfied air Mrs. McGregor wheeled about to collect Nell and Tim, who were already tugging at her skirts. She felt as if the events of the past half-hour were a dream. Carl, her harum-scarum son, the catastrophe worker of the family, was the acknowledged friend of Mr. John Coulter, one of the richest and most revered citizens of Baileyville. And more than that he appeared to possess the influence to have men removed from their jobs and discharged employees reinstated in lost positions. He even had power to have people's salaries raised. Would wonders never cease?

CHAPTER XIX

UNRAVELING THE SNARLS

How late the McGregors sat up talking that night it would have been alarming to confess. It was so late that the streets became silent and deserted and conversation had to be conducted in whispers lest it arouse the O'Dowds, Sullivans, and Murphys.

And what tense, eager whispers they were!

Mrs. McGregor, her bonnet still in her lap, sat on the edge of a chair too engrossed to so much as think of the shrimp pink tulle dress she had planned to finish before she went to bed that night; nor did she, in her usual methodical manner, take time to slip out of her best skirt or put away her company shoes and gloves. She was far too excited for that.

Happy, tumbled, and nodding the babies had been put to sleep and afterward their elders, joined by Hal and Louise Harling, huddled in the kitchen, closed the doors, and talked and talked. Every detail of Carl's amazing story had to be told over and over again that his listeners might enjoy to the full the marvel and humor of each successive event. Everything was clear as crystal now—Corcoran's transfer, Louise's reinstatement, Hal's increasing salary, the Christmas dinners. Even the conundrum of the watch remained an enigma no longer.

"It was, of course, Mr. Coulter who told Corcoran about your rescuing his baby," Carl explained to his chum. "I remember that I happened to mention the accident to him."

Hal nodded.

"But the thing I don't understand," he said with a puzzled air, "is how you could go to that office looking for a job and never so much as suspect who Mr. Coulter was. There must have been signs up with the firm's name on them."

"I suppose there were," Carl answered. "I don't know about that. You see, I was too rattled and wrought up to notice much of anything. Besides, I was some scared. It was such a swell joint and that bell-boy (or whatever you call him) was so lofty and elegant that it froze the blood in my veins. More than that I was crazy to get a position and was so darned afraid they wouldn't take me that I wasn't thinking of anything else."

"You're a bully little pal, Carl," Hal remarked, placing an affectionate hand on the younger boy's shoulder.

"Pooh! I did no more than you'd have done for me if I'd been in a hole," replied Carl modestly. "You'd move heaven and earth to help us if we needed you."

"You've said it, youngster!"

"Then what is there so remarkable in my trying to do the same for you and Louise?"

"It was splendid of you, Carlie," whispered Louise.

"Oh, I didn't do much," was the gruff retort. "As it happened, I didn't really do anything. But I wanted to—you can bank on that."

"Evidently you convinced Mr. Coulter of the sincerity of your good intentions," grinned Hal.

"Mr. Coulter! Gee! Every time I think of him I have to laugh. Picture my having the nerve to go reforming his mill for him and complaining of his employees! And fancy me parading into his private office asking him for work! Had I known what I was doing I should have been petrified with fear." Smothered laughter convulsed the boys frame. "Well, as Ma says, ignorance is bliss and fools rush in where angels fear to tread."

"I guess Mr. Coulter sized up the situation all right," mused Hal.

"Oh, he knew; he understood the whole thing. He told me so to-day," Carl responded quickly. "He's live wire enough not to let a joke slip past him. He had his fun out of the affair and don't you think he didn't. What's more, he didn't mean ever to let me find out what a boob I'd been. He was just going to keep the secret to himself. Then this wedding party came along and he happened to think we might like to come. So he took a chance and sent the bid."

"And that explains why the invitation came to you," reflected Mrs. McGregor.

"That's it, Ma. You have your little son Carlie to thank for your card to the spree," the lad responded impishly. "I'll be getting you into high society some day if you're good."

"If you don't get us all into jail or some other place before then we'll be lucky," came brusquely from his mother.

"Now isn't that gratitude for you?" growled Carl with mock indignation. "Here I take my mother and all her family to a perfectly good party and this is all the thanks I get for it."

"Yes, this happened to be a perfectly good party," agreed Mrs. McGregor mischievously. "But it might have ended in some scrape or other and like as not it would another time. One never can be sure where your adventures will bring up."

"Well, Ma, Mr. Coulter appreciates me if you don't."

"Apparently he does—up to date. Just you take care that you go on deserving his good opinion."

"I mean to," Carl flashed. "Say, folks, sha'n't we have something to write Uncle Frederick now? I'll bet it will take ten sheets of paper to retail the whole thing; and then he won't really have any idea of what happened. None of you ever can. You just ought to have been there and seen the play."

"It's as good as a play—as good as any moving picture, in my opinion," Louise ventured.

"What wouldn't I have given to be under the seat of that car and listened when you were laying out poor old Cork!" Hal ejaculated.

"I laid him fine and flat," acknowledged Carl with candor.

"Events have proved you did. Poor Cork! Still, Corks float, you know, and he has. He isn't dead yet by any means," jested Hal. "In fact, he told me only a day or two ago that he liked his new job much better than he did the old one so I guess nobody need waste pity on him."

"I'm afraid he wasn't punished much, after all," sniffed Mrs. McGregor.

"Oh, he's had it borne in upon him that he was a brute, Ma; don't you fret," declared Carl. "Mr. Coulter never does things by halves. When he starts in he finishes up a job in bang-up style. Corcoran's learned his lesson; and if he has that is all that is necessary."

A clock struck softly.

"Hal Harling! Do you realize it is twelve o'clock?" Louise exclaimed in dismay. "We must go home this minute. The very idea of our staying here and keeping the McGregors up until this hour! I'd no idea it was so late. Why, you may be robbed of your precious Corcoran watch if you don't hurry home out of the lonely streets. Good-night, everybody! And blessings on you, Carlie! You've been a trump. I'm going to begin to-morrow and work harder than ever for Mr. John Coulter."

"Here's to him!" Carl began. But a restraining hand was clapped over his mouth.

"Carl! Carl! For mercy's sake, remember that it's twelve o'clock and everybody's abed and asleep. Don't go cheering for Mr. Coulter now. You can go out in the field and do it to-morrow."

"I'm afraid I'll be too busy to-morrow."

"And what'll you be doing to-morrow, pray, that's of so much importance?"

"Why, I'll have to be deciding whether I want to go to college, or go to sea with Uncle Frederick; or go into Mr. Coulter's mills," was the teasing answer. "I seem to have three careers open to me. Maybe I'll have to toss up a penny to find out which I'd better take. Will you lend me the penny, Ma?"

"Indeed I won't," snapped his mother wrathfully. "Three careers! Humph! Still I'm not saying that if you could go into the mills with Mr. Coulter to stand behind you you might not make your fortune. But there's time enough to decide that later. We needn't argue it at twelve o'clock at night."